it's not easy
being bad

Also By Cynthia Voigt

THE BAD GIRLS SERIES
Bad Girls
Bad, Badder, Baddest

THE TILLERMAN SERIES
Homecoming
Dicey's Song
A Solitary Blue
The Runner
Come a Stranger
Sons from Afar
Seventeen Against the Dealer

THE KINGDOM SERIES
Jackaroo
On Fortune's Wheel
The Wings of a Falcon
Elske

OTHER BOOKS
Building Blocks
The Callendar Papers
David and Jonathan
Izzy, Willy-Nilly
Orfe
A Solitary Blue
Tell Me if the Lovers Are Losers
Tree by Leaf
The Vandemark Mummy
When She Hollers

It's not easy being BAD

by Cynthia Voigt

AN ANNE SCHWARTZ BOOK

ATHENEUM BOOKS FOR YOUNG READERS
NEW YORK • LONDON • TORONTO • SYDNEY • SINGAPORE

For Molly Hartman
(Bad Girl, Ret.)

Atheneum Books for Young Readers
An imprint of Simon & Schuster Children's Publishing Division
1230 Avenue of the Americas, New York, New York 10020

Book design by David Caplan
The text of this book is set in Janson Text.

Printed in the United States of America

2 4 6 8 10 9 7 5 3 1

Library of Congress Cataloging-in-Publication Data
Voigt, Cynthia.
It's not easy being bad / by Cynthia Voigt.—1st ed.
p.   cm.
Summary: Two unpopular girls try to break into the seventh grade clique system,
even though they're not really sure they want to be popular at all.
ISBN 0-689-82473-4
[1. Popularity—Fiction. 2. Schools—Fiction. 3. Individuality—Fiction.
4. Friendship—Fiction.] I. Title
PZ7.V874 It 2000
[Fic]—dc21   99-087807

FIRST
EDITION

Contents

1

Miss Very Unpopular and Miss Almost As

"What's so bad about me?" Mikey Elsinger demanded.

Two weeks after the start of seventh grade, she and Margalo Epps were wandering around outside West Junior High School, with maybe five minutes, maybe seven—or maybe only four minutes left until the bell rang to summon them to homeroom and the start of another day's uneasy boredom.

Margalo reminded her, "You don't *want* to be friends with any of these people."

Mikey just repeated her question. "Do you know what it is about me?"

Margalo did have a few ideas on the subject. They'd been best friends since the first day of fifth grade, and she'd seen the effect Mikey had on other people—sort of like the effect Godzilla had on Tokyo. But Margalo also knew human nature and she had figured out by now that when somebody asks you what's wrong with them, the thing they really don't want to hear about is: what's wrong with them.

Besides, she didn't think the things other kids didn't like about Mikey were *wrong* things. They were just Mikey, like her thick braid and her short, solid, quick-moving body, the bossiness, the never-backing-down, the not-listening, the only-seeing-things-her-own-way. Mikey was a one-way street, with a high speed limit. No wonder her life was full of collisions. Margalo really admired Mikey, and envied her, too. Sometimes. About some things.

The two girls wandered up to the main entrance and wandered into the building; they drifted down a broad hallway crowded with seventh and eighth graders, leaning against lockers, clustered in small circles, talking about sports and TV shows, griping about parents, all the time watching one another watch one another. Nobody paid any attention to Mikey and Margalo. Just about anything, two gerbils, a pair of potatoes rolling down the hall, anybody was more interesting than Mikey and Margalo. Becoming nobodies as soon as they walked into the first day of seventh grade was one of the things Mikey and Margalo liked least about junior high.

"Sometimes," Margalo said to Mikey as they moved along unnoticed, "I feel like I come from another planet."

"They're the ones from another planet," Mikey said. "I hope a meteor gets it."

Turning a corner, they entered the broad central hallway, its walls painted a soothing beige, its floors a thick, sound-muffling linoleum. Here, throngs of seventh and eighth graders moved in both directions. "I *asked* you," Mikey said. "Don't tell me you don't have ideas, because I know better."

West Junior High was all on one level, with the cafeteria, auditorium, and library located in the center of the building. Because it was central, the library had no windows. But it did have tables, and a thick carpet if you preferred sitting on the floor. It was the library they wandered into now. "I *asked*," Mikey said again.

"Well," Margalo answered slowly, trying to think of what she might say that wouldn't set Mikey off on a rant about how Margalo spent too much time thinking about what other people were thinking (which Mikey definitely did not do), or how people in general were chickenhearted sheep (which Mikey definitely wasn't), the same speech Margalo had heard a hundred times before, and did not want to hear again. Even if Mikey was right, Margalo didn't have to listen to her rant about it. "Look at it this way . . . ," Margalo said, even more slowly, wondering how long she had before the bell rang and rescued her from this conversational predicament.

Mostly, people worked together at library tables, comparing homework, preparing excuses. A few of these people Mikey and Margalo knew from their old school. Hadrian Klenk was alone, hunched over one of the computers behind the stacks, but Ronnie Caselli was at a table with a group that also included Derry Zurlo and Tanisha Harris. Tan wore a hooded sweatshirt, which declared athletics as her interest, and Derry wore a logo-ed cotton polo like Ronnie's, except in a different color. The new girl, Frannie Arenberg, was at the same table.

Everybody was new to West Junior High School, and Frannie was new to town, too, so she was an entirely new girl, but she was already one of the most popular seventh graders. Seeing her, Margalo was seized by inspiration. "Take Frannie," she said to Mikey, who glared with a toothy smile at the table of girls. "You're about the exact opposite of Frannie."

Mikey studied Frannie, who was—like almost every other seventh-grade girl—medium tall, medium thin (or medium fat, if you wanted to put it that way), medium pretty, and nothing special except for having great hair. Frannie wore her golden brown hair long and whenever she moved her head, it swayed and flowed like hair in a TV ad. Unlike other seventh and eighth graders, except Mikey, Frannie had bangs that feathered down over her forehead. But bangs were about all Mikey had in common with the new girl. Frannie Arenberg smiled a lot, big bright smiles as if she was having a good time in seventh grade, and she laughed easily, a real laugh, not a screechy seventh-grade-girl giggle. From day one, everybody had known who Frannie was—the new girl—and everybody wanted to be friends with her.

"What's so special about *her?*" Mikey demanded. She hadn't bothered to lower her voice, so everybody sitting at that table looked up.

Mikey wasn't about to look away from those faces.

Ronnie gave Margalo a little quick smile, the kind that doesn't want to be smiled back at, and Tanisha raised one waggling finger to Mikey, *Shame on you.* Mikey flashed back an *I-could-care-less* smile. The rest of the girls looked blank, even Derrie, as if they had never seen Mikey and Margalo before. But Frannie Arenberg smiled right at them, her big, round, brown eyes happy to see them. She moved her chair over, offering them room at the table with everybody else.

Luckily, the bell rang.

"What's *wrong* with her?" Mikey demanded as they left the library.

After homeroom, Mikey and Margalo separated for their morning classes. Margalo was in the A English section and the C math, and she felt worried to have been placed even that high in math. Mikey's first two classes were nonability grouped, social studies and gym. Then Margalo went to her gym class, which seemed ability grouped to *her*, and social studies, which definitely wasn't, while Mikey had B English and A math. They usually managed to meet up at their lockers at least once in a morning.

Not that they had anything particular to say. Just, they could have someone to talk to who wanted to talk to them. It was lucky for them that the basic organizing principle of junior high was the alphabet, because that put them in the same homeroom, the same lunch, and the same humanities seminar.

That morning, Margalo did have something to say

as they clanged their locker doors open, shifting books and notebooks, checking papers. "I'm your friend," Margalo pointed out.

"You don't count. You *like* me," Mikey explained. "I'm talking about friends, we're in seventh grade, friends are people you go to the mall with. Not people you like. They're people who when other people see you with them everybody thinks you're an okay person. They're people you act with the way I promised myself I'd never act."

"That's a joke," Margalo decided.

"Friends are people to hang with," Mikey concluded as another bell rang and they joined another surging crowd, which moved them away from one another.

The next time they met at the lockers was before first lunch. Margalo had been thinking. "People to hang *out* with," she said.

"You are such a schoolteacher," Mikey argued.

"People to hang with is, like, hanged by the neck until dead," Margalo argued back.

Mikey knew that the person with the last word wins. "That's what I mean," she said.

Margalo took out her lunch bag and slammed her locker door shut. They went to the cafeteria.

Mikey did *not* enjoy her cafeteria lunch, a slab of meat loaf covered with brown oobleck, an ice-cream scoop of unnaturally smooth mashed potatoes, peas so pale, you knew they had spent the last days of their lives locked away in some can. Mikey swallowed quickly, with minimum mouth exposure to what she was putting into it.

"You should eat from the salad bar," Margalo advised. Her lunch was a bologna sandwich on supermarket whole wheat bread, pale and pasty brown but an improvement over Aurora's usual supermarket white bread. Margalo also had a banana, and there was nothing much you could do to ruin a banana, and saltines with peanut butter. Only a few seventh and eighth graders brought their lunches from home—vegetarians, kosher kids, kids with allergies. It was definitely not cool to BYO for lunch at WJHS, but Margalo's family consisted of three sets of siblings, plus her only-child self, plus Aurora and Steven, whose marriage brought together so many people. In Margalo's family, money was tight, so she had no choice about brown-bagging lunch.

Mikey had a choice, but she didn't like it. "The salad bar lettuce died last week," she told Margalo. "In some foreign country. After a long illness. Lunch

8

is the only time I miss having my mother around, you know? That woman packed a great lunch."

"She probably still does," Margalo pointed out unsympathetically.

"Well, dunhh. But not for me."

"You could pack your own lunches," Margalo pointed out unsympathetically.

"I could. Maybe I will. If I do, don't think I'll share with you."

"Okay, I won't think it. But you will. You'll want me to tell you how good it is."

Mikey denied that, although she knew it was true. "Dad will tell me."

"But you won't believe him the same way you will me, because he's your dad and he thinks everything you do is terrific."

"Not everything," Mikey said, but the protest was insincere. Her life had actually gotten a lot easier since her parents separated, and her mother moved back to the city. Everybody had benefitted from the Elsingers' divorce. Mrs. Elsinger had a new position with improved prospects for promotion, and she didn't have to sneak around to see her boyfriend. Mikey and her father moved out of their fancy neighborhood into a more modest house and were banking most of the child support checks into Mikey's new college account. Even Margalo had benefitted, since Mr. Elsinger paid Aurora, Margalo's mom, to take responsibility for Mikey until he could pick her up. Between Mr. Elsinger's money and Sam's Club, Aurora and Steven were getting by more easily.

Mikey pronged four peas and held up her fork. "These cafeteria lunches make an educational contrast to our home cooking," she said, claiming, "that's the only reason I eat them," which Margalo didn't believe for a minute. Mikey rotated her pea-tipped fork, studying it. "They used to put the heads of executed criminals and traitors on spikes near the Tower of London," she told Margalo, then put the fork into her mouth. There was no need to chew. This was a mush-and-swallow eating event.

Margalo looked around the big cafeteria. Tables of seventh-grade boys, tables of seventh-grade girls, and tables where the boys and girls sat together, which meant they were eighth graders. No seventh grader was ready to eat lunch with a boyfriend or girlfriend, no matter how many hours they might spend together at the mall practically on a date.

Mikey also looked around. "Last year wasn't like this," she said. "I liked last year."

Margalo was happy to share some of her ideas about the many differences between sixth and seventh grades. "Last year, with one teacher all day, in the same classroom all day, people had to act the way the teacher wanted. Now we're split up into all different classes with different teachers so we're on our own more. Being on our own makes most people nervous, so we band together, like in clubs." Margalo enjoyed explaining human nature to Mikey (who wasn't all that interested in the subject, except when it got in her way) so she added, "Besides, if you're a club you get to exclude people."

"We should start our own club," Mikey said, looking around at the tables.

"A club of two?"

"You know what I mean."

"I know what you mean to mean," Margalo allowed. "And I don't agree with you."

"So what else is new?" Mikey said, to win the argument.

"*Zut!*" Margalo muttered, short for *zut, alors!*, which was French. Before school started, Mikey had decided that one thing they shouldn't do was swear, "because everybody will expect us to be really foul-mouthed." Margalo agreed, except, "You have to say

11

something, sometimes, or people will think you're a wimp." So they were developing their own cuss vocabulary. Mikey's grandmother in California, who dyed her hair red, used to say *zut, alors!* whenever Mikey captured one of her chess pieces. Mikey and Margalo put that first on their list of cuss words, followed by *rats!* (stolen from Snoopy), and *mice!* (derived from *rats!*), and then (by natural progression) *rodents!* Margalo was thinking of *bunnies!* She was waiting for the chance to try *oh, bunnies!* out on Mikey.

"Then we should be a clique," Mikey suggested.

"Cliques have to be something people want to be in."

"Why shouldn't I be popular?" Mikey asked.

Margalo just shook her head. In Margalo's opinion, the words "Mikey" and "popular" didn't even belong in the same dictionary, much less the same sentence. Typical, normal kids were what worked in junior high, as far as Margalo could see, but she didn't bother pointing that out to Mikey.

"Is it the way I dress?" Mikey asked.

"We never talked about clothes before seventh grade," Margalo pointed out. "That's another difference."

Mikey stuck to her point. "*You* don't dress like anybody else, either. Although you always look—like some model in *Elle*? Not like *Seventeen*. Like some exchange student. Or someone from another planet," she added. "I think it's because you're so tall, and skinny. You look better dressed than other people, even if you do get all your clothes at thrift stores."

"And the New-to-You," Margalo added, ignoring the reminder that she was one of the tallest people in the seventh grade, boys included. Actually, she thought it was lucky she couldn't afford to dress according to fads. Because of that, she dressed according to her own sense of style, wearing calf-length skirts as often as jeans, wearing blouses not T-shirts as a rule, and never cute little tees over cute little minis, even though those, like everything else, looked good on her. Mikey was short and round and already a C cup; she wore wide-legged cargo jeans and gray T-shirts, the same thing every day, her going-to-school uniform.

"Even if we dressed like them, we wouldn't fit in," Margalo said now. "But you could try, if you cared what you look like."

"How do you know I don't care?"

"Because if you did, you'd do something about it."

"What makes you think you know all about me?" Mikey demanded. "But even if I dressed like one of

13

the jockettes," she said, "or, better, like a Barbie—it still—"

That picture caused Margalo to practically choke laughing. The Barbies were what they had named the girls who wore big heads of curled hair, or some other designer hairdo, like beads, any hairstyle that took hours to create. High-maintenance hair was a hallmark of the Barbies. Also, they dressed in full skirts with wide, tight belts, shoes with spindly heels. And they wore full-face makeup, every day. Mikey didn't even *own* a pair of dress shoes, or a lipstick.

"It's not that funny," Mikey said, and hoped the time was right to ask, "Want to trade your banana for this chocolate pudding?"

Margalo didn't.

Mikey didn't ask again. Instead, she explained human nature right back at Margalo. "It's much easier for boys to be popular, because they're almost all jocks. Even if they're good at school, they're still jocks first. But with girls—it's more complicated. There are all these specialized groups, jockettes, punkers, arty-smarty types, as well as the Barbies, and let us not overlook the preppies." Mikey stopped to think about what she had said, before concluding, "Then there's us."

"What about us?" Margalo asked.

"We're some subcategory of normal," Mikey decided. "Not regular normal. But whatever kind of normal we are—sub-, or ab-, or even super- —mostly we're *not*."

"I am," Margalo maintained.

Mikey snorted sarcastically.

"Closer to it than you, anyway," Margalo claimed, and then admitted, "I *look* closer, and how you look is what counts in seventh grade."

Mikey went right on with her own idea. "But practically every one of us not-normals has maybe one friend. So maybe each pair of us *is* a clique after all. I don't see why we can't be. You could be wrong about something, Margalo. And I *could* get popular."

"I'll *share* the banana with you," offered Margalo, who'd had a sudden glimpse of how things would be if Mikey wasn't around to eat lunch with. "How would you go about getting popular?" she asked.

And then Mikey surprised her. "I'm going to give it more time," said Mikey the impatient. "Think about it, Margalo, it's taken us almost two weeks just to find our way around the building, and in sixth grade some people ended up liking us, didn't they?"

"Everything's different in seventh grade. Everybody. School's different."

"How much could people who were all in grade school last June have changed, in just four months?" Mikey demanded. "They can't scare me."

At that moment, when Margalo's mouth was jammed full with banana, a bunch of girls streamed by their table, including Derry and Annaliese, in J.Crew sweaters over jeans. Margalo watched them, keeping her mouth closed. The little installment of preppies went on by without a word, but Frannie Arenberg hesitated, and stopped. "Hey, Mikey." She smiled down, including Margalo in her brown-eyed cheerfulness.

"Hey," Mikey mumbled through her own mouthful of banana.

"Frannie?" Frannie's friends called back to her. "You coming?"

"Hey, Margalo," Frannie said.

Margalo nodded a little nod, smiled a little smile, and waited. Then Frannie hurried off to catch up with the others, and Mikey muttered, "A real Little Miss Merry Sunshine, isn't she? It's like having a cocker spaniel around."

"More like a golden retriever," Margalo suggested.

"What's *with* her?" Mikey demanded.

"Maybe she doesn't know any better? Or maybe

she's friendly. Maybe she's a nice person," Margalo suggested.

"Yeah, yeah," Mikey said. She gathered her trash onto the tray. "What my grandmother calls a good egg."

"Which is another name for somebody who is no fun at all."

"You *would* say that. You're a bad egg."

"Well, so are you." Margalo stuffed crumpled wax paper and the banana skin into her brown bag, getting up, picking up her notebook and texts.

"Being a bad egg doesn't mean I can't get popular," Mikey said. "Or, at least, more popular than you."

"Not a chance."

A challenge was just what Mikey liked. It gave her something to do, and something to win. "Oh, yeah?"

"Not that being more popular than me would make you particularly popular," Margalo pointed out.

"I bet I can," Mikey warned, promising.

"But you don't care if people like you," Margalo reminded her.

"Neither do you."

"Yeah, but I'm a better liar." Then Margalo added, "You know, it's not really being popular I want. I just want not to be *un*popular."

That was it, exactly, which Mikey hadn't known until Margalo said it. "Me, too," she said, but didn't say what else she was thinking: about how if she didn't have Margalo for a friend, her school days would be about a zillion times more boring. Instead of that, what Mikey said was, "How can you tell if you're popular? Otherwise," she explained to Margalo's surprised face, "how will I know when I am?"

2

Can Bad Eggs Make Good?

"*H*ere's the plan," Mikey announced, about two weeks later.

"Plan for what?" It was raining, a cold, early October rain, so they had gone to the library after lunch. The big room was crowded, and noisier than the librarian usually allowed. The doors to the tutoring rooms all stood open, and people had gathered there, too, horsing around, talking, watching one another.

Mikey and Margalo wandered along the stacks, as if they were looking for something to read, which they weren't, since Mikey almost never looked for anything to read and Margalo used the town library to keep the pile of books beside her bed tall enough. "Plan for me getting popular," Mikey said. "Frannie already likes me."

Margalo didn't say anything.

So Mikey went on, "But Frannie likes everybody, so she doesn't count. It's sort of depressing how nice she is. D'you think it's because she's a Quaker? D'you think I ought to be nice? D'you think I ought to be a Quaker?"

"I don't think you *can* be nice," Margalo said, and Mikey reached up to hit her on the top of the head with the flat side of her big loose-leaf notebook.

"Do you want to hear the plan or not?" Mikey demanded.

"Go ahead, shoot. No, don't shoot. Please don't shoot—tell." It always cheered Margalo up to get on Mikey's nerves.

"I'm going to have a party. A Halloween party."

"Leaping lizards, Mikey," Margalo said, to buy some time. "Holy cow." Nobody would want to go to any party Mikey gave, especially on Halloween. This was a bomb of a plan. It was doomed to total failure. Margalo tried to think of how to convince Mikey not to do it, and when she realized that would be impossible, she tried to think of ways to distract her. She asked, "How old do you think is too old to go trick-or-treating? Esther wants to go, and Aurora says I have to take her, but I think she's too old. I know *I* am. Are you?"

"A dinner party."

Margalo tried again. "What do you think the chances are that parents will complain about the religious paintings in seminar? Nobody did about the Greek statues and they were nudes, but some people might about religious pictures."

"I'm a good cook. I'm the star of home ec."

"People do get excited about religion," Margalo went on, speaking slowly, and thoughtfully. "Of course, they get excited about sex, too."

Mikey realized: "But if you take Esther around you won't come to my dinner party!"

"Maybe they think *nude* and *sex* are synonyms," Margalo said.

"A dinner party will make them like me," Mikey told Margalo, with a smirk of victory.

Margalo gave up, and pointed out, "You can't make people like you."

Mikey ignored that. "How about Mom's lasagne?"

"It's great."

"No, beanbrain, I mean what if I serve that at my party?"

That Mikey wouldn't listen if you didn't agree with her was a given, as they say in math. Margalo had never been able to talk Mikey out of anything. All she could do was hope that Mikey would get bored with the idea, and drop it.

Besides, if Mikey insisted on giving a party, that wasn't Margalo's problem, and maybe it wasn't even any of her business. Besides also, Margalo had other things to think about right now. She was building herself a reputation at West Junior High School. First it became commonplace for her to arrive at school and be commented on. "Looking good," or, "Where'd you get those socks?" She kept her style simple and—of necessity—kept it cheap. "Really retro," they said, and Margalo smiled to herself because if they knew where she shopped they'd know she was weirder than they might already think she was, and pitiful, too—two surefire roads to deepest unpopularity.

Lately, some people had started asking her opinion, about a haircut, an accessory, a neckline, or a color choice, and when they did, she gave one. Mostly, Margalo would say what people wanted to hear, but she'd also stick in a little advice, the raisin in a bite of cinnamon sweet roll. "How about a funky pin?" she'd suggest, because pins got noticed, and add, "Your skin looks great with yellow, doesn't it?" She never criticized directly. Who wanted to hear, "Cripes, that green makes you look like you just escaped from a mortuary"?

Not any seventh-grade girl, that was for sure.

Unless, maybe, Mikey, because then she could get angry at how opinionated Margalo was, and how Margalo didn't know everything even if they were going to vote her Miss *Mademoiselle* Magazine of the Year. Mikey would be just as likely to explain why she *wanted* to look like a mortuary reject, and how if Margalo had two brains to rub together, she'd have already figured that out, but she thought she was so smart, didn't she. Just because she always looked good.

Just thinking about what Mikey might say made Margalo grin.

The real difference between her and Mikey was that Margalo couldn't afford to be as different out loud as she was silently, to herself. She was going to need scholarships for college, if she wanted to go to college—and she did because that was a requirement to get a good job. She knew that for scholarships you needed lots of activities, clubs and publications and community services, which meant getting along with people. Getting along with people meant them thinking you were no different from them.

Just because you weren't normal didn't mean you had to flaunt it. Even if she thought Leonardo DiCaprio was prettier than Claire Danes, she wouldn't say that to anyone; well, no one but Mikey. Even if she thought Mrs. Brannigan, their humanities seminar leader, was the best-informed teacher she had, Margalo wouldn't say that to the girls who made fun of the way the teacher dressed. The girls liked to exclaim about how Mrs. Brannigan had been dumped by her husband for the girls' basketball coach last summer. "Just, how embarrassing! I'd die! I'd never come back to teach here," a Lindsey would say, and a Heather would answer, "But she doesn't even notice. That's probably why it happened; she doesn't notice anything. Look at the way she dresses; she doesn't even notice what a total dog she is."

But, *what was wrong with dogs, anyway?* Margalo would be privately thinking. Dogs always looked good enough. They just looked like what they looked like. And there was certainly nothing wrong with being way smarter than these toads and turkeys, Margalo thought, keeping it in the animal kingdom as she bobbed her head up and down, just like all the other girls, "Uh hunh, uh hunh," and giggled like them, too. Sometimes, Margalo wished she was like Mikey, and couldn't even see the way things really were, so that she wouldn't have to spend so much time trying to convince people that she wanted to be just like them.

Now Mikey asked her, "Do you think I should serve lasagne for the dinner? If not, I could do chili. My mother has a good recipe for chili. I could serve it with rice and corn bread, or the lasagne would have Italian bread, and tossed salad with both. What do you think?" Mikey asked again, as if she would ever listen to any suggestion Margalo made. "For dessert, something light—probably a good idea if we're going out for candy, later."

Candy? Trick-or-treating? Big mistake, Mikey, Margalo thought to herself. *Not at all cool.*

"I'm telling everyone to come in costume," Mikey concluded.

"Who have you invited?" When everybody declined her invitation, Mikey would have to face reality, and cancel.

"Nobody yet. I'm mailing the invitations. They're RSVP, Regrets Only, and I'm designing them on the computer. I'm not all that good yet with the graphics program," Mikey admitted. "Or I could make pizzas, but those are a lot of last-minute work, and besides the best pizzas come from a pizzeria."

"When did you turn into such a cook?" Margalo asked, trying again to change the subject.

"When my mother left home. What would you do, chili or lasagne?"

Margalo wouldn't do either, because she wouldn't be having a dinner party if she was Mikey and it was Halloween, and it was seventh grade.

"You aren't very enthusiastic," Mikey pointed out.

"I'm not sure it's such a good idea," Margalo responded at last. Added to everything else, she'd also heard about a couple of other parties the same night. Rhonda Ransom was giving one, and one of the Heathers had an uncle with a barn that they were turning into a spook house. Ronnie reported that her cousins and all their friends were going to spend the night running around town, egging car windows and front steps. Louis was going to egg Mr. Saunders's house, Ronnie said—or his car; or maybe both—to get even with the principal for picking on him in the first assembly. Ronnie told Margalo that she was going to Rhonda's party even if Rhonda was the hostess.

"Linny's going, too. I'm going as Cher. I think. I found a black wig I look sort of great in." She giggled.

"Plus, you've got a great body," Margalo had said, which was what Ronnie hoped to hear.

"Not really," Ronnie had protested feebly. "Anyway, all a good body means is that guys harass you. Say things, grab you, you know?" Margalo didn't. "So you have to watch your back a lot," Ronnie explained. "Either that or go around like Mikey, looking like some—sack of flour."

"Maybe you should try that, if you're so bothered."

"I think I'll just stick as close to Franny as I can," Ronnie said. "Nobody hassles her. You're so smart, Margalo, do you know what it is about her?"

She asked but before Margalo could answer, Ronnie had gone on in a rush of words, "I never see you anymore. Let's see more of each other. Gotta go," and she ran off to join Heather McGinty, who was passing by in the midst of her clique like some cruise ship surrounded by tugboats.

Remembering that, and because she *was* Mikey's best friend, Margalo gave her some unsolicited good advice about her plan. "You know, Mikey, maybe you shouldn't give this party. You haven't mailed out the invitations yet, have you?"

They had left the library now and were on their way to humanities seminar, the junior high enrichment program for the best students, where they were about to start a Renaissance unit.

Mikey looked around for eavesdroppers before she answered, "I'm mailing them Monday. Mom said that about two weeks in advance is the right timing."

"If you haven't invited anyone, why don't you wait until later?" Margalo asked. "To give your party."

"This is the best time for me. I don't want to do New Year's, that's for sure. And Valentine's Day is out. I mean, who wants to celebrate Valentine's Day? At our age."

"But what about your birthday? What about *my* birthday?"

"Is that what you're after? You want me to give you a birthday party? Well, too bad, Margalo. I don't want people to like me just because I'm your friend. Just because I'm your—sidekick. I'm not anybody's sidekick. *And* I've got our bet to win."

Margalo repeated her main point. "The party's a bad idea."

"Thank you for your support, Miss Know Everything Better Than Me, but don't worry about it. I won't invite you."

"You know I have to take Esther around."

"Then why are you trying to ruin my party?" Mikey demanded.

How Mikey's brain worked was a mystery to Margalo. Here Mikey was, eating cafeteria casserole—pale, maggoty macaronis mixed with strawberry pink tomato meat sauce, topped by a stiff layer of yellow cheese, with burned bread crumbs over it all—shoveling it into her mouth as if she didn't mind it, at the same time as she was fussing over a fancy menu for her dinner party.

"I want an impressive dessert; dessert impresses people," Mikey said. "What do you think?"

"I'm not the home ec expert," Margalo said. She was *not* going to get sucked into this conversation as if she'd changed her mind about what a bad idea the party was.

"For the main course, maybe I'll have Julia Child's Boeuf Catalan," Mikey concluded. "That was one of Mom's best dishes, and you can do it ahead, too."

"If your mother liked cooking so much, why did she leave her cookbooks behind when she left?"

"She said she was tired of being a full-time mother. Well, I was tired of it, too, I can tell you that."

"But she wasn't. She always had her job, even when you were little, didn't she?"

"Whatever," Mikey said. "That's why we got the cookbooks and the vacuum cleaner. Mom took the silver, of course, but then she's always had a good eye for value."

"Aurora's the one who's a genuine full-time mother," Margalo pointed out.

"Anyway, I'm using the cookbooks, so it's not like they've been abandoned the way me and Dad were."

"Hairballs, Mikey. It's only a divorce. You've been set free, not abandoned."

Mikey smiled a *Getting-away-with-it* smile. "You could say that." Then she had a sobering thought. "If my mother figured that out, she might come back!"

"Not likely," Margalo said. "It's not like her to retrace her steps. Return to the scene of the crime."

"I like her better divorced, anyway."

Margalo peeled four long yellow sections of skin from her banana.

Her home life situation settled, Mikey returned to

real concerns. "Then what about Boeuf Catalan, you remember that one, don't you? It's stew with rice cooked in; you loved it. You *will* help me get ready, won't you? Sunday morning?"

Margalo didn't want to have anything to do with this doomed dinner.

"Although, you're not much use in the kitchen," Mikey added. "Maybe you'd better clean the house. You're good at that."

A couple of days after Mikey mailed the invitations, Frannie Arenberg approached Mikey and Margalo's cafeteria table. "Is it okay if I sit here?"

Margalo shrugged, smiled, and wished she had some more distinguished sandwich than peanut butter and jelly on supermarket white bread.

Mikey considered the question, staring up at Frannie.

Frannie looked at Mikey's face and just laughed. "It's only one lunch," she said. "I don't bite."

"I might like you better if you did," Mikey remarked.

Frannie laughed again. She sat down facing Margalo and Mikey. "I can't come to your party, Mikey. I'm sorry."

"Oh. Oh, well. No problem," Mikey said, and squeezed open her milk carton, jamming in the straw.

Frannie and Mikey had identical lunches on identical trays: two pieces of fried chicken, one ice-cream scoop of rice, and a bright yellow puddle of corn.

"Anybody want some pb and j?" Margalo asked, offering to share because it was the kind of thoughtful thing a nice person did; but she should have known better, because "Absolutely," Mikey said, and took half of Margalo's sandwich. Frannie did what you were supposed to and said, "No, thanks," although Margalo would have bet money—if she'd had any money to bet—that Frannie did want it.

"These are the worst lunches I've ever had at any school," Frannie said, then, conversationally.

"Me, too," Margalo agreed. "I mean, they look like the worst I've ever not had."

"But I was home schooled for the last couple of years, so maybe the field went into a decline while I was gone." Frannie ate her chicken with a fork and knife, not with her fingers. Margalo made a point of not staring at this breach of manners. Mikey didn't.

After a while, Frannie said, "My father home schooled us."

"Doesn't he work?" Margalo asked.

"Yes, but at home. He does people's taxes. The schools were so bad in the last place we lived, we'd have been put ahead, and my parents didn't want us to be the youngest in our classes."

"Like Hadrian Klenk," Margalo said.

"Hadrian doesn't have much fun at school," Frannie agreed.

She and Margalo talked away easily, and Mikey ate.

"What does your mom do?" Margalo asked.

"She gets businesses back on their feet, when they're in trouble. They hire her to tell them what's going wrong, and why, and how to get things going right."

Mikey spoke. "A management consultant?"

Frannie nodded.

"I thought you were Quakers," Mikey objected.

"Friends have always been successful business-people," Frannie said. "Because of being so practical."

"Friends?" Margalo asked.

"That's what Quakers call themselves, the Society of Friends."

"Did you like home schooling?" Margalo asked. "Or did you miss being with other kids?"

"I had my three sisters, and I saw other kids at the weekly meeting. My dad's a good teacher. He knows just about everything. So I liked it. The only problem is, I didn't take any of the standardized tests regular schools give in sixth grade."

"That's why you're not in a seminar," Margalo guessed.

"You could have taken the tests at the public schools when they were being given there," Mikey pointed out.

"I'm not complaining," Frannie said.

"Okay," Mikey said. "You're not. So what do you want from us?"

"*Zut,* Mikey, *alors!*" Margalo protested.

But Frannie didn't take offense. "You're both in Mrs. Brannigan's seminar, and that's the one I want to sit in on. The school is giving me a two-week trial period, to see if I'm a good enough student to take seminar. Can you believe it took all this time for my parents to persuade Mr. Saunders just to let me try? And that's *after* we finally got an appointment, so we could argue our own case."

"Why us?" Mikey asked.

"I want to know what you think of her."

"But why us?" Mikey repeated.

"Because you think for yourselves," Frannie explained. "Everybody else gossips about her, but if you

34

two like her, she's probably a good teacher. Do you like her seminar?"

"It's okay," Mikey said. "For school." Her attention returned to the chasing of kernels, which skidded around the plate trying to escape her Terminator fork. "We're about to start the Renaissance."

"I know. I wish I'd been there for Greece. Did you read the myths?"

"Literature's not until next year," Margalo said. "But we heard about Schliemann's excavations. Even Mikey liked Schliemann. You can admit that, just to us, Mikey."

"Everybody told him he was wrong," Mikey explained, "and he wasn't."

Frannie went along with this conversation as if they *were* friends, the three of them, and knew each other. "So, can I go to class with you for the trial period? What are you reading, or are you doing art now?"

"Art this week," Margalo said. "Next week we're talking about *The Prince*."

"Machiavelli," Mikey announced. "I'm looking forward to Machiavelli."

Frannie shook her head. She'd never heard of him. "I just don't want to go in alone. I know it wouldn't bother you, Mikey, but it does me. It's okay, isn't it, Margalo? If I stick with you two?"

"As long as you don't stick too close," Mikey answered, and that set Frannie off again. "You laugh a lot," Mikey observed.

"People are pretty funny," Frannie explained.

"You mean they're ridiculous," Mikey corrected.

"Yeah, sometimes that's what I mean," Frannie agreed.

3

One (bad) Egg, Scrambled

The Monday morning after Halloween, Margalo waited outside for Mikey's bus, so she could hear about the party, who talked to who about what, how they liked the food, and if—against all probabilities— Mikey had been transformed into a popular person. The day was sunny and crisp, a clear blue sky over the flat roof of the school, people standing around in their down vests and Polartec vests, or their heavy knit sweaters and hooded sweatshirts. Margalo waited for Mikey, and a few people greeted her as they got off buses, "Great sweater."

It was an old Irish knit, an Aran sweater someone had discarded because of a couple of big holes. Margalo had paid fifty cents for it and sewed up the holes;

now she looked like someone out of a PBS special about Ireland. Or Scotland, maybe, somewhere overseas where people were exotic and more interesting.

Finally, Mikey came down the steps of the bus, in her cargo jeans and a green and white jacket, looking a lot like a brussels sprout.

A brussels sprout having a serious attack of bad temper, Margalo realized. Mikey emanated a force field of fury so strong that everybody was giving her a lot of room, and looking back at her over their shoulders. Mikey smiled a *Don't-even-think-of-it* smile, more warning than friendliness, more threat than warning.

Margalo considered going somewhere else, maybe the library, maybe the cafeteria, to join up with other people for the rest of the day.

Or maybe the rest of her life.

But instead she sidled up next to Mikey. "Hey," she greeted her.

Mikey didn't respond, not even to the extent of looking at Margalo. Margalo didn't have to be a mind reader to get the message: *Get lost, why don't you?*

With all of the step-siblings and half siblings Margalo dealt with, she knew lots of ways to start a conversation with somebody in a funk. You could ask, "What's wrong?" with just the right amount of sympathy in your voice, or you could remark, "You look cheesed off," which avoided bad language but still sounded lively. You could be direct: "Want to talk?" Or indirect: "I've got a problem I hope you can help me with; is this a good time for you?" You could blatantly ignore the person's mood, and get points for understanding that someone didn't want to talk about it, by saying, "The *Titanic* sank because of faulty rivets; did you know that? It's true, I read it in the paper." You could even try a bad joke, like, "How many teachers does it take to change a lightbulb?"

Usually, Margalo was pretty skilled at handling people, but Mikey, well—Mikey wasn't people. Mikey was Mikey. And Mikey was looking at the West Junior High School students as if she were an alien from another universe, whose eyes could kill off any carbon-based life-forms that happened to be in range. Whose smile was a death ray.

Her glance fell on Margalo. "What's so funny?" she demanded, but she didn't wait for an answer. "They're not going to get me," Mikey promised Margalo. "There's only sixteen hundred and fifty days left until we graduate from high school," Mikey said grimly. "Not counting snow days. I can make it for sixteen hundred and fifty more days."

Margalo would never question Mikey's math. She walked along beside her friend, walking fast.

It had to be the party, of course. Something had gone wrong at Mikey's party.

"Everybody thinks because they're on top, they can get away with anything," Mikey said. "But I'm not about to go along with that. No way, no where. For example, have you realized that they keep seventh graders off school sports teams? Even if they're better than the eighth graders? Like me in soccer, if West had a girl's soccer team. Or Tan in basketball."

Margalo had longer legs than Mikey, but when Mikey got going, Margalo had to scurry to keep up. She didn't remind Mikey that whatever the school policy might be, Mikey took tennis clinics on weekends, and was already a serious contender at the county level, so she wasn't exactly competition deprived. Besides, Mikey wasn't talking about sports, anyway; Margalo was pretty sure of that. Margalo was pretty sure this fury was about the party.

"They don't know who they're up against," Mikey announced.

That, Margalo would never argue with. When they got to their lockers, she reached into her lunch bag and brought out a peanut butter cup. "For you from Esther," she said.

Margalo knew that peanut butter cups were Mikey's favorites and she thought that however much Mikey groused about it, she liked Esther's acting as if Mikey was some Michael Jordan-Xena combination. So when Mikey looked like she was about to refuse Esther's gift, in order to keep feeling totally bad, Margalo said, "Or I'll eat it."

"You'd like that, wouldn't you?" Mikey answered grimly as she took the candy and unwrapped it, and devoured it in three swift bites.

It was a simple enough question, but by lunchtime Margalo still had not figured out how to get it asked. She could wonder, "Exactly how bad was it, Mikey?" Or, "So, how did the party go?" Or she could try an indirect inquiry—"Y'wanna hear about my Halloween?"—which would naturally lead into an exchange of Halloween reports.

Margalo stood behind Mikey in the cafeteria line, watching her tray fill up with a wide bowl of vegetable soup, and a sandwich of grilled cheese so skinny, it resembled some cartoon coyote a ten-ton weight had fallen on, a container of milk, and a little bowl of quivering red Jell-O. All around them people were talking, but Mikey just glared down at her lunch as if she planned to torture it first, and then kill it. Following Mikey to their usual table at the far end of the cafeteria, Margalo decided that she was just going to have to ask point-blank, like firing a gun: "What went wrong with your party?"

But it turned out she didn't have to. They were about to climb over the bench to sit in their usual seats, facing out, backs to the wall, when Heather McGinty, head preppie, her little short skirt swishing—swish, swish—her loyal followers close behind her, walked in front of their table. And stopped.

The followers mostly wore little short skirts like Heather's, or loose trousers that tied at the waist; they all wore little short T-shirts under little short misty gray or misty blue or misty green cardigan sweaters. They liked socks with designs on them and clunky shoes, although none of them went as far as Doc Martens. All of them had shiny clean hair and pinky-brown lipstick, and they waited, bright-eyed and eager as a herd of chipmunks, waiting for Heather to exercise leadership.

Heather looked at Mikey with an *Oh! it's you! What*

42

a surprise! expression on her face. A big, fake *Oh! it's you! What a surprise!* expression.

Mikey had one foot on the bench and held her tray out in front of her. Her expression was furious.

Nobody even noticed Margalo, who was sort of impressed that Heather hadn't backed off when Mikey first glared an *If-you-knew-how-much-I-don't-like-you-you-wouldn't-be-standing-there-you'd-be-running* smile.

"Hey," Heather said, drawing it out. "Mikey," she said, the way you say the name of someone you've just been thinking—or talking—about.

Mikey didn't say a word.

Heather had pulled her hair back with a band, so that when she turned her head to look back at her preppies-in-waiting, you could admire her profile, with the little straight nose and the little round chin. Her preppettes answered with excited giggles or smirks, each according to her own character and taste.

They knew something was coming, Margalo could see that. They knew something was coming and they knew what it was. This was the way people worked in cliques; everybody knew, so that they could look forward to it, beforehand, and really enjoy it, during, and talk it over, after.

"You probably don't know Mikey Elsinger," Heather

said to her friends. The friends watched Heather, not Mikey. "Mikey's the one I was telling you about, who sent out those really funny invitations, as if she was giving a formal dinner party, as if she was really inviting me—me and Heather James, and you, too, Annie, you got one, didn't you? and—oh, you know, everyone. That was a cool joke, Mikey."

Beside Margalo, her foot balanced on the bench, her tray balanced in her hands, Mikey waited. Without saying a thing.

A fake concerned expression floated over Heather McGinty's face and settled there, a hen settling down on its eggs. "It *was* a joke, wasn't it?" she asked, so sincere that everybody had to know she was faking.

There was half a minute or so of silence. Then the girls around Heather started to laugh, and people at nearby tables turned around to see what was going on.

Even though she didn't want to, Margalo couldn't help feeling embarrassed, and ashamed to be Mikey's friend. And that made her angry, too, and ashamed—again! double ashamed!—to chicken out on Mikey, and furious at Heather McGinty, too, for making her feel this way.

Things were easier for Mikey.

She took her foot down, off the bench.

She shifted her grip on the tray.

She flipped the tray, sending her whole lunch flying up, spraying chunky soup and skinny sandwich, and milk, and Jell-O, out across the table, so it could rain down over Heather McGinty.

And all the time Mikey was smiling furiously.

The preppettes twitched back, chipmunks in retreat.

Heather stood there with her own tray in her hands, dripping vegetables off her little round chin, a couple of red Jell-O chunks sliding down the front of her little short tee, which used to be misty gray. Her pinky-brown mouth was open in protest, but she didn't seem to have anything to say.

"Joke," Mikey said, her teeth bared in a smile. "Get it?"

Then she strode down the aisle and across the cafeteria and out through the wide doors. Margalo followed.

Out in the hallway, Mikey slowed down to a walk. "You'll have to share your lunch with me."

"We're not allowed to eat—"

"We'll be by our lockers. Nobody'll even notice. I can't get through the afternoon without something in my stomach." Then Mikey laughed. "I feel so much better—she looked like she got sick all over herself, didn't she? If I were her, I'd make me sick."

"Mikey, what happened?" Margalo demanded as they went down the hallway to their lockers.

"You were there," Mikey explained. "I threw my lunch at her."

"Rats on it, Mikey, I mean yesterday. I mean your party." Margalo took her sandwich out of her bag, packaged ham with mayonnaise and lettuce, on supermarket white. She gave half to Mikey, who chomped down on it, and chewed, swallowed.

"Bad ham," Mikey said. "Lousy bread. Yellow mustard. Can't you do anything with Aurora? Nothing happened," she concluded.

"What do you mean, nothing?"

Mikey went into sarcastic mode. "Let's see. What does nothing mean?" She tugged at her braid as if trying to pull the answer out of her head. "I guess it means zero. Zip. The big goose egg. It means, not one thing. Happened," Mikey said, her fury building up again. "Not one person. Came. I cooked, you cleaned, we set the table, Dad was out in the kitchen ready to be my sous-chef, serve up the plates . . . and after a while we realized that nobody was going to show up."

Margalo didn't know what to say.

"*And*," Mikey added, "I missed the Sunday tennis clinic." She continued adding to the pile of wrongs done to her. "Which means I also missed two hours of playing time, after."

Margalo held her chewed bit of sandwich in her mouth.

"Dad felt pretty bad," Mikey reported. She finished her sandwich half and held out her hand for the paper bag. Margalo passed it to her. Mikey said, "Probably the worst moment of my life. So far. The most humiliating, probably. Is it okay if I take the apple?"

Margalo nodded.

"I figure," Mikey said, crunching on the apple, "they did it on purpose. They got together and didn't come. But they didn't even call to say so. I said on the invitation, Regrets Only."

"There *was* another party yesterday, at Rhonda's. And one of the Heathers had a party, too," Margalo told her.

Mikey took in that information. "You didn't tell me."

"Would it have made any difference if I had?"

"We'll never know, now, will we?" Mikey asked. "But *you* wouldn't just totally blow off an invitation, would you?"

Margalo was shaking her head, no, and no, she would never.

"See? And you haven't even got anybody to teach you good manners," Mikey told her. "I wrote it on the invitation, Regrets Only, and my phone number." She finished the apple and looked into the bag again, pulled out a packet of Oreos, and asked, "You don't want any of these, do you?"

Margalo shook her head.

"Well, they've had their chance," Mikey announced. "They've had their one and only chance with me. At least, now that's settled, I can stop trying to be popular. I can just concentrate on getting through the next six years any way I can."

"You really think you've been trying to get people to like you?"

Mikey wasn't listening. "You weren't invited to Rhonda's, were you?" she demanded.

"I'm the last person Rhonda would invite."

"No, you're not. I am. You're second to last. Second best, second to me. I win again."

That was when they saw the principal coming down the hall toward them. Mr. Saunders was a big, broad man, part African-American, part Native American, with large hands and no gray in his curly hair. The story about him was that he'd been scouted by the Celtics but had gone into the army for the college loan program. He used to be a coach, before he became an administrator, and he always wore a bright blue and white warm-up jacket over his button-down shirt, never a suit jacket. Now, he bore slowly down upon the two girls. Margalo quickly took her lunch bag and jammed it into the locker. Mr. Saunders had told them at the first assembly that nothing got by him and nobody could fool with him, because he'd been a coach. He made a point of telling them that, he said, "So you boys will know where I'm coming from."

Margalo slammed the locker door shut just as she was figuring out that by acting guilty she would make Mr. Saunders suspect that she had something to hide, like drugs, or liquor, which she would never be so stupid about, but how would he know that? She thought about opening her locker up again so he could see they'd only been eating lunch illegally, but by then he loomed over them.

"Michelle Elsinger?" he asked, looking from one to the other.

"Yes," they answered together.

But there was no way Margalo could convince

Mr. Saunders that she deserved to go back to the office with him, too. In fact, she only asked once because his refusal was so large and loud a NO that it took all her nerve to look slowly over at Mikey, shrug, and say, "See you later."

Mikey went off at Mr. Saunders's side, glaring up at him with unconcealed fury.

4

Junior High Justice

"*You* don't think I'll end up pregnant, do you?" Mikey demanded.

Margalo had been on a slow boil all afternoon, thinking about those dinner guests, and in homeroom at the end of the day she'd taken the first chance she'd had to ask Mikey what had happened with Mr. Saunders. And this was all Mikey could say? "I think you'll be lucky to end up married," Margalo answered.

"You can get pregnant without getting married," Mikey reminded Margalo.

"Crikey, Mikey." Margalo watched Mikey's eyes narrow at the cute little rhyme and then said, "Ask a stupid question, get a stupid answer."

"He thinks I will."

"Who?"

"Mr. Saunders. He said so," Mikey said. "After he told me I'd have to apologize to Heather, and I told him he couldn't make me. But he *knew*, Margalo. He knew all about my party. So everybody must know, so she must have told everybody. But he figured out pretty quickly that if he tried to make me apologize, he'd end up having to expel me. He's a smart guy."

"Mr. Saunders thinks you'll get pregnant and you say he's smart?"

"It's what rebellious girls do. He read it in a book: Antisocial boys get violent; antisocial girls get pregnant."

"Boys *can't* get pregnant. That's the only reason they don't," Margalo observed.

"He said he looked up my record and he knows all about me," and Mikey grinned. "That means he looked at yours, too."

Margalo stuck to the point. "If it's not to apologize, what *is* your punishment?" This was their first real run-in with junior high justice, and she was curious.

"I have to help clean the cafeteria after first lunch for the rest of the week."

"Maybe Mr. Saunders is okay," Margalo said.

"Or maybe he doesn't think girls merit big-time punishments," Mikey answered. "Maybe he doesn't think a girl can get up to anything all that disruptive. That's my guess, anyway. Remember the first assembly?"

"You mean with Louis Caselli?"

"All Louis did was lip off a little, and Saunders was all over him."

"Get real, Mikey. You know what Louis is like."

"But it was the first assembly, and all Louis did was say, 'Yes, SIR,' the way they do in the army, in the movies. But Mr. Saunders gave him the works, don't you remember? The silent stare. The leaning over the podium. The calling by name." She quoted, "'Lou-is Ca-sel-li, if I'm correct,'" in a deep, looming voice.

"But in the end, all Mr. Saunders did was say he didn't share Louis's sense of humor," Margalo made her final, winning point and smiled. "I remember perfectly."

Mikey made her own winning point. "This afternoon, he didn't even know at first if I was me or if I was you. He started out school knowing the boys' names, especially the troublemakers. But he hadn't even looked at the girls."

"He's not supposed to be looking at the girls."

"You know what I mean."

"It was a joke," Margalo said.

"Not very funny."

"It is, if you have a sense of humor."

"He doesn't respect girls," Mikey said. "He doesn't think we'll give him any trouble. He doesn't even think we *can*. Do you think he's right?"

"It's never girls who get national headlines," Margalo admitted. "But in that case, you'd think he'd respect us *more*."

Mikey followed her own train of thought. "Because things really are different in junior high. We're all getting different. You are, too."

"You're not," Margalo pointed out.

"I was about to," Mikey admitted.

It took Margalo a minute to figure this out. She asked, "The party?"

"The"—and Mikey interrupted herself—"it's really lucky that what happens in junior high doesn't mean the rest of your life will be like that."

"Yeah," Margalo agreed.

"Because otherwise, ninety percent of the people in the world would have killed themselves by now."

"Mikey," Margalo asked, light dawning, "exactly who did you invite? Besides me."

They were seated on the bus, Mikey beside the

54

window because Margalo had had it Friday. Mikey looked out the window, watching kids filing into the other buses as she listed off all the names in a low voice. "Heather James, Annie Piers, Stacey Beard, and Lacey Gleason and Tracey Tomlinson. Linny Mitchell, and Tanisha, and Ronnie. Rhonda Ransom. And Frannie."

Margalo honed in like a heat-seeking missile. "Rhonda Ransom? You asked *Rhonda Ransom?* Why would you do a thing like that?"

Mikey shrugged, avoiding looking at Margalo, avoiding the question.

"Because she's popular this year? And you know that's just because she's turned into a Barbie with the way her figure—"

Mikey shrugged and kept looking out the window. The bus pulled away from its space at the curb.

Under cover of the grinding gears, Margalo didn't have to lower her voice to state the obvious. "You hate Rhonda Ransom."

Mikey's shoulders shrugged.

"And she hates you."

Shrug.

"What was it, did you pick out the most popular girls?"

Shrug, shrug.

They were silent for a couple of stops until Margalo said, "So now we know about our old friend Ronnie Caselli, and our old friend Tanisha Harris. Linny never liked us, anyway, so she doesn't count."

"Don't feel sorry for me," Mikey warned her.

"I don't. You were pretty stupid, if you ask me."

"I didn't ask you."

"Well, you should have."

"But you told me you couldn't come."

"You know what I mean, Mikey. But I thought Ronnie was okay, and Tan, too. I really did." Margalo wasn't used to being wrong about people.

"We're in seventh grade now, remember?" Mikey explained.

The bus surged, and stopped, unfolded its doors and let people out. Then it pulled in its signs and turned off its lights, and surged along again.

"Especially Tan," Margalo said.

"Hairballs on all of them, Margalo," Mikey decided. "They don't matter. Not to me, anyway. Not anymore."

Mikey sounded like she meant what she was saying.

"I mean, I spent the last six weeks trying to pass as normal so I'd be acceptable to these people. I feel like

I had the six-week flu, or went temporarily insane. No, I mean it, now I feel—after this party—like I've been let out of a cage. I didn't even know I was in a cage, Margalo, I didn't even know I was sick. Boy, do I feel better," Mikey said.

If it was a sickness, wanting to be liked, wanting to fit in and mix in, then Margalo had it. But not, she realized, because she wanted to *be* popular. What she actually wanted was people *thinking* she was popular, so that it would be easier to *be* Margalo.

Most people didn't want you to be yourself, and now they were trying to get at Mikey because Mikey couldn't be anything else. But Margalo wouldn't let them get away with that, and she bet Mikey wouldn't, either. "What are you going to do now?" she asked.

"There's a fifteen-and-under tournament this weekend," Mikey said. "Five clubs are signed up for it, lots of players, and that means I'll get lots of matches."

"*I* mean to get even with them," Margalo said, "and so should you."

"I already did," Mikey said, and went back to what interested her. "There'll be both doubles and singles matches. Probably, I'll win both. I'm developing a slice serve—you want to come watch?"

Maybe Mikey didn't want to think about it, and Margalo could understand that, but she'd find ways to get them, especially Tan and Ronnie, who were at least supposed to not be Mikey's enemies.

And Rhonda. It was always fun getting back at Rhonda.

And that snotty Heather McGinty, her too.

Margalo was cheering up. This would give her lots to think about, especially if she planned not to get in trouble over it; and that *was* her plan. A good revenge had to be out in public, like Mikey's humiliation was, so that everybody would know. Also, a good revenge was one where the revengee knew better than to try to get even back. Also, a good revenge would show people they couldn't get away with trying that kind of trick on Mikey and Margalo.

5

The Revenge of
the Ant People

*I*t turned out that Mikey did sometimes take Margalo's advice. The very next day, Tuesday, Heather McGinty once again had food splatter over her as she waited in the cafeteria line when Mikey, already served, passing by, stumbled, tilted her tray as she tried to keep from losing her balance, and happened to dump her lunch all over Heather.

"Oops," Mikey said.

On Wednesday, while Heather was carrying her tray over to join her friends at their table, Mikey happened to be going by in the opposite direction, and happened to swing her arm to show Margalo how John Travolta danced in his old movie. Heather's tray flew up into the air and covered her arms and chest in slices of hot turkey, and the gravy the sandwich was smothered with, and the dark red cranberry sauce that was served on the side; then it clattered onto the floor.

"We have to stop meeting this way!" Mikey cried.

A few disloyal giggles could be heard.

After the first attacks, Heather McGinty could never be sure what might happen. She took to keeping a clean shirt and sweater in her locker. She took to hovering in the center of a circle of friends whenever she was in the cafeteria, like the nucleus of an atom.

Meanwhile, Mikey had also gone up to Tan and Ronnie, to tell them to their faces, "You stink, both of you."

"Heather told us it was a joke, didn't she, Tan?"

"You know I don't have any sense of humor."

"We thought you'd changed, didn't we, Ronnie?"

"Why would I change?" Mikey demanded.

"Because it's junior high," they explained.

Margalo, who was watching this, almost laughed out loud.

"You're lying," Mikey told the two girls. "You don't expect me to believe that you believed Heather McGinty, do you?" she asked.

Tanisha, in jeans and a sweatshirt, studied the toes

of her Nikes, but Ronnie stuck to her guns. "And why shouldn't we?"

Mikey didn't bother arguing the point. "You've turned into total wimps, doing whatever Heather tells you." For a long time she stared right into Ronnie's face; then she aimed her hostile glance right at Tanisha.

"This is really stupid," Ronnie said, but Tan admitted, "Maybe we wanted what she was saying to be true."

"Because you wanted to go to Rhonda Ransom's party," Mikey told them. "You total toadstools."

"You just want to boss everybody!" Ronnie said.

"Rats on that, Ronnie. I just want people to call up and say they aren't coming to my party, when I've invited them Regrets Only, and they aren't going to come."

"All right," Tan said. "We will."

"As if I'd ever ask you again," Mikey said.

After Tanisha and Ronnie walked off, Mikey turned to Margalo and mimed twirling a pair of six-guns around her fingers, then returning them to imaginary holsters. "Not too shabby, was I?" she remarked, with a smile that asked its own question: *Aren't I something?* Then she said, "What are you going to do about Rhonda, Margalo?"

Margalo could surprise people, too. "I'm already doing it. You mean you haven't noticed?"

Margalo's revenge on Rhonda was subtle, but it didn't take Rhonda long to figure it out. When Margalo slipped in among the big-haired girls, and sidled up to greet her—"Hey, Barbie, how's it going?"—Rhonda was immediately alarmed, just a flash of fear, like a rabbit startling at the sound of a dog's bark. Then she sniffed and turned away, as if she hadn't even heard Margalo, and couldn't see her, anyway.

Margalo repeated the greeting two or three times that first day. On the next day, she called across the gym to Rhonda, "Yo, Barbie! What's happening?"

People turned to see who this Barbie was, since there was no Barbie in the gym class. They began to make the connection. "Why does she call you Barbie?" Rhonda's friends asked her. "Did you change your name for seventh grade?"

"No, I didn't," Rhonda said, "and I don't know why. She's just some dork from my old school. Nobody liked her; she's not normal."

When Margalo saw Rhonda talking to an eighth-grade boy in the cafeteria, she moved in without hesitation. Rhonda was winding her hair around a finger and smiling up into his face, flirting, being flirted with, and knowing that everybody who saw her was jealous.

Margalo approached from the direction Rhonda was facing, a big fake smile on her fake friendly face. "Hey, Barbie," Margalo greeted her.

Rhonda's cheeks turned pink with anger. "That's not my name and you know it!"

"And I see you brought Ken to school with you today," Margalo said, passing them by.

She heard laughter spreading around, the way ripples of water circle out when you drop a penny into a wishing well. She pretended not to notice.

Ken—or whatever his name was—backed off from Rhonda like she'd tried to kiss him or something, and she tossed her head of big hair before she flounced off to join her formerly jealous friends.

Margalo joined Mikey at the table.

"I'm saving my coleslaw for Heather," Mikey told her.

"You ought to eat the coleslaw and give the hot dog to Heather," Margalo advised.

"I like hot dogs," Mikey protested. "Even boiled, like this, as long as there's mustard and onion—"

Margalo shrugged. You never could tell Mikey anything.

"What about Linny?" Mikey asked.

As soon as the question was asked, Margalo had the answer. "Linny's my new best friend."

First Mikey's face pinched with anger. Then she got it and "She should be mine," Mikey said.

"Why? It's my idea."

"Because I'm the one she'll hate having around the most. You could turn out to be okay, but I'm permanently out of it." As Margalo opened her mouth to say, *So what?* Mikey pointed out, "It's your own fault for being well-dressed," and then added, "You know I'm right."

Margalo shrugged. That day she was wearing a red-and-white-striped sweater over a calf-length black skirt, and she thought her shrug must make her look even more French.

Mikey didn't notice that. "You really know how to get people where it hurts, Margalo," she said, admiringly. "You really understand people."

"You could, too," Margalo told her friend.

"Maybe, but it would take too much time. And most people aren't worth the trouble. Except for you," Mikey said. "I understand *you.*"

"What makes you so sure about that?"

"You're like Machiavelli," Mikey said.

At that point, Frannie joined them at their table so they could go to seminar together, and asked, "Who's like Machiavelli?"

"Margalo."

"I don't think so," Frannie said, and turned her brown spaniel eyes on Margalo.

"You never think anything bad about anyone," Mikey pointed out.

Frannie didn't care about that. "Margalo wants people to like her, so she can't think it's better to be feared than loved. And that's Machiavelli's main point, isn't it? So you're the one like him, not Margalo."

Margalo was impressed. "She's right, Mikey. You're right, Frannie. I thought I was, but it's really Mikey."

"He was wrong, anyway," Frannie went on.

"Oh, yeah? Take a look at recent history," Mikey advised her.

Frannie didn't argue. "I know," she said.

"Or like gangs," Mikey added. "Even kids in gangs run people by fear."

Frannie pointed out, "It's no big deal, scaring people. Everybody can be frightened. But Machiavelli was saying was that it's better government to be feared than loved, and all I'm saying is, I don't agree.

Are you two ready to go to seminar? Because you haven't finished your coleslaw, Mikey. Unless you're going to dump it on Heather? Or is this a dumpless day?"

That inspired Margalo's next revenge. It was easy steps from dumpless to dumpling, from dumpling to the Miss Dumpling Award, and from that to the Little Miss Muffin Award.

Margalo only included Mikey in the planning of this final revenge because she had to, but she had to admit that with the two of them working on it, it improved. Mikey had her dad's computer graphics program, and a color printer, so the award certificates looked pretty professional. "They're terrific," Mikey informed Margalo.

"You always think that what you do is terrific."

"Usually it is."

"You're pretty cheerful these days," Margalo remarked.

"It's a load off my mind not trying to be popular. And what's so funny now, Margalo Epps?"

"You. You are." She changed the subject. "These certificates are going to look great."

"All we have to do now is find out which lockers—"

Mikey started to say, but Margalo was way ahead of her on that. "I already did. It wasn't exactly high espionage, Mikey. You just watch people."

"I've got better things to do."

"Oh, yeah? Like what?"

"Like right now, trying this on a yellow background. Yellow or orange, what do you think?"

Margalo thought yellow, against which the image they had made contrasted well, the plump, white, bubble-headed muffin wearing a jolly red-lipstick smile and happy half-moon eyes with long, stiff eyelashes, with its stick-figure legs under the pink ruffled skirt of its muffin cup. The certificate was pretty simple, like all good advertising graphics. It had a blue ribbon border ending at the bottom of the page in a blue first prize rosette. The merry muffin on its long dancing legs appeared at the middle of the page, slightly below center. Below her was a slogan Mikey and Margalo had argued over until they both liked it: THERE'S NOTHING MORE SWEET AND SMILEY THAN MY MORNING MUFFIN. And along the top ran the title: THE LITTLE MISS MUFFIN AWARD.

Against the bright yellow background, the bright red title in 24-point Old Gothic font would be readable from yards away, as their awards greeted Heather,

Annie, Stacey and Lacey and Tracey, and Linny, especially, because Linny had changed from being a not-stuck-up queen of their sixth-grade class to being someone who wouldn't even say hi to you if you weren't in some in-group. Margalo's job that morning was getting those six award certificates taped up on the six lockers, and herself to gym not suspiciously late. She was in such a hurry, she didn't even stand back to admire their work.

Later, Margalo didn't have a chance to stand back and admire, because there were groups of people crowding the hall, reading and laughing; either that, or watching the papers being ripped off and ripped up, and laughing.

Mikey and Margalo arrived from different directions, so they had to watch the scene separately. "I think the real winner is Linny," some boy said. Another argued that Heather was the roundest, most muffin-like, and another that Tracey had the most stick-like legs. "But Linny's the one who dances like that," insisted the first boy.

This turned into a chanting, cheering contest—"Miss Muf-fin, Miss Muf-fin, Miss Muf-fin"—with rhythmic clapping, and each candidate with her own group of supporters, both boys and girls. "Sta-cey,

Stacey," battled with, "La-cey, La-cey," for airspace, while one group maintained, "Annie's eyes, Annie's eyes."

The six contestants were bunched together in the center of all this, trying to look like good sports, looking to one another for reassurance, trying not to be caught getting angry, or weepy, or embarrassed. "Ha, ha-aha, ha, ha," they pretended to laugh.

"Who—?" they muttered to one another, and, "Where's—?"

Heather McGinty leaned over to whisper something into Annie's ear, and Annie's eyes swung to Mikey like a compass needle finding north. "Mikey," she muttered to the other five, and Mikey smiled right at them. *Gotcha!*

Margalo watched Rhonda Ransom slip up beside Heather McGinty, big blond hair next to sleek blond style, and whatever Rhonda said to Heather, Heather looked at Margalo and didn't believe it. Margalo thought she knew what Rhonda was saying, and if Heather McGinty had asked Margalo's advice, it would have been, "Believe it."

Gradually, the group dispersed to all show up late for their next classes, temporarily unconcerned with getting into trouble, because they had all—with six exceptions—been having such a good time. Mikey and Margalo exchanged a satisfied glance and went their separate ways. They could have made more copies and kept posting and re-posting the award certificates, but Margalo had convinced Mikey that once was enough, once was the way to do it, once would get exactly the ongoing humiliation that Margalo and Mikey hoped for.

So that when Rhonda turned on Margalo in gym the next morning, shrieking like some demented mother whose children won't behave in the supermarket, her eyes filled with tears as she cried out, "You're ruining my life!" when all Margalo had done was ask, "How's it going, Barbs?"—that was the end of their revenges.

They had gotten even, and maybe a little ahead.

But what Mikey didn't ask Margalo, and Margalo didn't ask Mikey, although both of them wondered it, was this: *That probably blows it for both of us, don't you bet?* Neither one of them needed to say out loud to the other, *I'm not a bit sorry.* They both already knew that.

6

The Cheese Stands Alone

Mikey arrived at school the next morning ready for a fresh start. Not a fresh start at being popular—or even a fresh start at being less disliked. No, she was finished with the whole popularity question. What difference did it make, anyway, if people liked you? She couldn't think of anything she wanted that being popular would make it easier to get. Being unpopular could make it *harder* to get certain things, she did understand that. But she wasn't convinced that *harder* was an insurmountable obstacle.

And, besides, she didn't have anything against obstacles. In fact, she kind of liked them. So as long as she had Margalo for a friend, Mikey was as popular as she needed to be.

Mikey did understand that it wouldn't be quite as

71

easy for Margalo. Margalo *had* been sort of quiet on the bus going home the day before, and her voice had been sort of little on the phone last night, when she said the few things she had to say. But Mikey had been feeling more and more energetic, and had lots to say, the more she thought out what was bound to happen after what they had done. Mikey's opinion was, people could dislike her as much as they wanted now that they knew they couldn't ignore her.

In fact, Mikey would prefer *not* to be someone people liked.

She hopped down off the school bus, eager to explain this to Margalo, and convince her how great things were going to be, from now on. Halloween was behind them and Thanksgiving only a couple of weeks away, and it was a cold, gray November morning with a few little flurrying flakes of snow drifting down in the air. Her grandmother had called to ask could she fly over and spend Thanksgiving with her only son and her favorite granddaughter, to which both Mikey and her father had said, "Yes! Great!" Then Mikey's father had asked, if he hadn't been the only son, would she have gone to a brother's instead; and Mikey had demanded to know why she wasn't the favorite grand*child*; and Mrs. Elsinger had cackled away on her end of the phone while they cackled back at her.

So things were looking pretty good, Mikey thought, looking around for Margalo—who wasn't there.

Mikey went inside to find her. It could be that Margalo's bus was late, but it might also be that Margalo was too cold to wait outside for Mikey because she hadn't yet gotten herself a winter jacket, or whatever she was going to wear that year. Margalo could probably come to school wearing an old blanket pinned at the neck with a baby's diaper pin, one of those big pins with a yellow duck on the end, and she'd look good. Mikey thought she'd tell Margalo that.

Mikey went to the library and stood inside the door, looking around, but she didn't see Margalo. Nobody noticed Mikey; at least, nobody looked at her, or smiled at her. So she went to the art room, where the arty-smarty clique spent their free time, and just stuck her head in. One or two people who didn't know her looked up, without any interest, and the rest ignored her.

You didn't think junior high was going to be warm and snuggly, Mikey reminded herself, going back to her locker. Because she was uncomfortable, as if the skin of her body didn't fit right, as if it were too tight, maybe. Or as if her skin were too baggy and loose, dragging around after her.

But where *was* Margalo? She wasn't at the lockers, either. Mikey went to homeroom.

When Margalo's desk was unoccupied, Mikey had to notice how everybody else was talking to somebody, and how nobody said anything to her.

Okay, Mikey said to herself. *So nobody in this room likes you. Big surprise.*

Margalo never showed up for homeroom, so that by the end of it Mikey had to admit that she was absent. And would probably not show up all day.

And hadn't called Mikey to warn her.

Mikey was angry, which was a lot more comfortable than being alone. Her anger got her to math, and once the teacher came in, everything was pretty much normal. One of the good things about teachers was: When they were running the room, the kids weren't. Another good thing was that teachers kept everybody paying attention, so if someone had something to say, even if she wasn't popular she got to say it, and at least one person—the teacher—would listen.

But Margalo had really dropped Mikey in the soup

by being absent, and Mikey wasn't going to forgive her easily; that was what was on her mind as she pulled books out of her locker, put books in, checked to be sure she had her homework, and went back to classes. Lunch, she was beginning to realize—going down the crowded halls in her own little bubble that everybody gave a wide berth to and nobody even looked at—would be the worst.

Standing alone in line. Crossing alone to her table. Sitting alone to eat.

Before she even went near the cafeteria, Mikey went to the pay phones in the hall just outside the main office. She put in her coins and dialed Margalo's number. As soon as Margalo said, "Hello?" Mikey let her have it.

"You could have called me," she said. "I didn't even bring a book to read."

"You don't read books, and there's a whole library, anyway," Margalo answered, as if she was the one who was angry. What did *she* have to be angry about? *She* wasn't the one stranded here, behind enemy lines.

"You know what I mean," Mikey said. "What's wrong with you, anyway?"

"Nothing."

"I mean, what kind of sick are you?"

"I'm not."

"Then why don't you come to school?" Mikey leaned her forehead against the cool silver metal front of the pay phone, not letting herself be distracted by the sounds around her.

"I don't want to," Margalo said, cross.

"Well, neither do I, but I'm here. And you didn't even call me up to tell me you were staying home."

"I couldn't."

"Why? Your hand was cut off in the night? Jeepers, Margalo—and why aren't you in school, anyway, if you're not sick?"

"I had to baby-sit Lily and be here for Stevie's car pool."

"What about Aurora, that's *her* job. Or Steven, if she can't."

"Steven has to work. Aurora had to go downtown."

"Downtown? Shopping? And you're baby-sitting? Talk about skewed priorities."

"Downtown to get Howie."

"Get him where?"

"From jail."

"What was Howie doing *there?*" Mikey demanded.

"He got arrested last night. Actually, this morning. The police picked him up on Threadwhistle Street—"

"But that's all private houses."

"I know."

"Private houses in a good neighborhood."

"I know. That's why the people there get nervous about loiterers. Especially teenaged boys. That's why somebody called the police."

"Why didn't the cops just bring him home?" Mikey asked, since this seemed to be why Margalo had to stay home.

"It was the third time," Margalo explained.

"The third time they picked him up? What is he *doing?*"

"There's a girl he's in love with. It's love."

"So he lurks around her house in the middle of the night? Real smart, Howie. Aurora should have left him in jail. You're missing a day of classes," Mikey pointed out.

"He's home now, anyway. She's giving him a bowl of soup. Canned chicken-and-rice. He's going to need a lawyer, and Aurora isn't sure his father will pay."

"Send him back to his father. He's no relation, anyway," Mikey argued.

"Aurora thinks he is. He thinks he is. He might as well be, I guess." Then Margalo changed the subject. "What did you have for lunch?"

"Nothing."

There was a silence from Margalo's end. Mikey waited.

"I *couldn't* call, Mikey. Aurora was on the phone talking to the bail person and lawyers, trying to find Howie's dad. It was pretty frantic here. I really *couldn't*."

"Okay, okay. Who's complaining? Don't get all worked up," Mikey said.

"How's school?" Margalo asked now, and about time.

Mikey didn't need anybody feeling sorry for her. "How bad can it be?" she asked. "What can they do, stick needles under my fingernails?"

She could hear Margalo smiling, and she smiled herself when Margalo said, "Does it count if they only want—really *want*—to?"

"What kinds of needles?" Mikey asked. Maybe she'd just talk to Margalo all through the long lunch period.

But somebody tapped her on the shoulder and said, "You're not the only person in the world, Elsinger."

Some girl whose name she didn't even know. Maybe even an eighth grader. Who cared? But there were several people waiting, and there were only two phones. Mikey hung up, but she was wondering: Why didn't the school have enough phones for the people who wanted to use them?

And she wasn't about to go into that cafeteria alone, either.

Margalo *should* have called.

The halls were empty because people were either eating lunch or in class. As Mikey approached her locker, she became aware of a stink. Not a nasty, rotten stink; a nasty *sweet* stink. Like the smell-advertising in those fancy women's magazines. Horrible perfumed air was floating around in the hallway near Mikey's locker.

Because the smell was coming right from her locker. And the front of it looked wet. She put out her fingers to touch it. Oily. Because somebody had sprayed some oily horrible perfume all over the front of Mikey's locker, and probably up into the ventilation slots, too; probably it was all over her books and papers, too.

Mikey opened the combination lock, and her guess was right.

Somebody—she understood this right away now—wanted to tell her she stank.

As if she cared.

But didn't dare tell her to her face.

As if, even if she did stink, she cared.

What chickens.

That was when Mikey became aware that she was no longer alone. She turned around slowly, to see who had showed up.

Lots of people, lots of familiar faces, lots of faces whose names she didn't know. Preppies and Barbies, arty-smarties and jockettes, and of course jocks, and of course, Louis Caselli's grinning baboon face. People from her old school, and people she hadn't even known existed until this year, and some people she'd seen—and scored goals past—on the soccer field, and a couple she'd played tennis against. What did they think she was, a circus show?

A satisfying anger was building up in Mikey as her smile, *You're-going-to-be-sorry*, fell on the faces at the front of the ring of faces. Rhonda next to Heather McGinty with tag-along Annie tagging along.

Mikey waited for her fury to hit the right temperature and then she went for the person standing right in front of her.

It was some Heather or some Lindsey, nobody she knew. But it was right there enjoying itself, that face, so Mikey dove for it, and punched, once, twice. Somebody pulled her off before she could land anything solid.

"What's she—?"

"What's *wrong* with her?"

"She's the same one who—"

The voices eddied around her, like waves, and she turned to face the person who had pulled her away, a boy. She thought he was in her math class, a brown-haired boy in a blue sweater, maybe his name was Tom. Or maybe she'd never seen him before.

As soon as he let her go, she gripped her hands together, palm to palm, fingers intertwined down beside her left thigh, and brought up a two-handed backhand stroke—and slammed him on the cheek.

He backed off, but he didn't back away. He raised crossed arms to protect his face, hands clenched, and stood his ground. Well, he was a good half-a-foot taller and many pounds heavier; if she'd been him she wouldn't back away, either. Mikey lowered her hands for a two-handed forehand swing at his other ear.

"That's not fair," he protested.

"As if," Mikey answered.

She saw Louis Caselli push his way up to the front row of a crowd that was chirruping in gasps, like muppets in a panic. "You come anywhere near me, Louis Caselli," she warned him, and he didn't.

"I don't hit girls," the boy she was fighting said.

"Hunh," Mikey grunted. But she unclasped her hands. "Okay," Mikey said, and he relaxed a little.

Which was a mistake, because she went after him with her feet, kicking his shins, stomping on his toes. She was wearing sneakers, but if you put enough ankle snap behind it, you could get a good kick off a sneaker. And if you had strong thigh muscles, which Mikey did, and you got up into the air a little, you could really stomp somebody's foot.

"Hey!" he protested. "Cut it—!" and he kicked back at her.

She danced out of his way. She was quicker than he was—until he landed his foot hard just beside her kneecap, so hard that she almost fell over sideways.

She swayed in a circle, to keep on her feet, balanced, and put out her elbows so that when she went back at him she could use both feet and elbows.

"Wow," somebody said. "It's feet of flame."

"Pull her hair! She hates that!"

"Man—is that chick coordinated or what?"

"Look out!"

But it was never clear who was supposed to look out for what, because Mr. Saunders had run up on the scene, and suddenly everybody started to be in a big hurry to be somewhere else. He put one hand on the boy's neck, ready to squeeze. "What seems to be the problem, Ralph?"

Ralph? Mikey had never heard of anyone named Ralph. What was this Ralph stranger doing trying to get into her fight?

"Nothing," Ralph answered. "Ask her," he said.

"She hit Heather!" a girl's voice cried.

"Heather didn't do anything!"

"Nobody did anything!"

"She hit Heather first!"

"I was just trying to stop it, sir," Ralph said.

Mr. Saunders let go of the boy's neck and turned his attention to Mikey. "Is that true?"

Why should Mikey lie? "Sure."

Mr. Saunders kept his eyes on her for a long minute, breathing in the smelly air. Then he said, "Come with me, Mikey."

Before she followed him down the hall, Mikey shut

the door of her locker and reset the lock. At least nobody was laughing anymore.

Mr. Saunders suspended her for the rest of the day, but he had to call Aurora to come take her away since her father was out of the office and not expected back until late afternoon. "I will deal with you tomorrow," he said to Mikey. "I want your father to bring you to school. Understood?"

"They stank up my locker," she told him.

"Who?"

She didn't know.

"You need to get your temper in control," he warned her.

"It is," she promised him.

"You need to learn how to get along with people," he told her.

"Does get along mean I do nothing when they stand around laughing because they stank up my locker?" she asked.

"You weren't asking for it?" he asked back. "You haven't been making fools of them? Don't complain when you get what you ask for," he told her. "I could suspend you for a week. How would you feel about that?"

Mikey was the first seventh grader to get suspension, and she was a girl. And she was about to leave for the day. The truth was, she felt just fine.

Mikey was prepared for the second part of the one-two combination punch, principal then parent. But "Ready?" was all Aurora said when she walked into the office where Mikey waited, her book bag at her feet.

Mikey—clearly ready and waiting—didn't have anything to say, either. They went down the hall and out the main entrance. Aurora had parked her old station wagon in the visitors' lot, so they had to pass a lot of windows, but Mikey didn't look up to see if any faces were looking out at her. She was thinking about getting what you ask for. She hadn't forgotten that the first thing she asked for was a simple RSVP, but that was just the specific cause. In general, if she had a chance to get what she asked for, she needed to think about what she really wanted.

She got into the front seat, strapped herself in, and made herself sit patiently while Margalo's mother backed cautiously out of her slot, as if the little sprinkling of snow hadn't melted away hours ago. Once Aurora was out on the street, safely in the right lane, slowing down in case any stoplight they were approaching might turn yellow, Mikey said, "Thanks for getting me."

"You're welcome," Aurora said. As if she didn't care how much trouble Mikey was in. "I assume you had some reason for fighting."

"A good reason."

"I don't know if I'd assume *that*," Aurora said. "But. You're your own problem, not mine. And your father's, and maybe a bit of Margalo's, too."

"Why Margalo's?"

Aurora pushed her hair back behind her ears, just like Margalo, and smiled to herself. "I'm glad Margalo has you for a friend," she said after a while, which might have been her answer to Mikey's question. "You've got broad vision." She turned her head to look at Mikey and added, "You know?" Then Aurora turned quickly back to face whatever might come at her from the road ahead. "I mean, you live in a wider world."

Mikey couldn't figure out what this meant.

"Like, you play tennis," Aurora explained.

"You mean I'm ambitious," Mikey said.

"It'll be easier for you when you're grown up. Out of school."

"Ambitious like my mother," Mikey said.

"Just because you're ambitious like your mother doesn't mean you're just like your mother. You're pretty fierce," Aurora told Mikey, as if Mikey didn't already know that.

"So's Margalo," Mikey said, in case Margalo's mother hadn't figured that out yet.

"I hope so," Aurora said.

Luckily, before Aurora could drive Mikey completely crazy trying to have a sensible conversation, they pulled up in front of Margalo's house. Mikey was out of the seat belt and out of the car before Aurora even had the keys out of the ignition. She had already decided how to tell Margalo about the day. "You should have called me," would be her first words. Right after, "What's for lunch?"

7

What Now? What Next?

"*I* need something to *do*," Mikey said to Margalo, about a week after the fight-suspension afternoon.

They were on their way to the auditorium. It was the second week in November, and civics had been canceled—again!—because of having an assembly—again!—for a seventh-grade class meeting. Wednesday, first period after second lunch, seemed to be the official assembly time.

Mikey and Margalo pushed their way to the front of the seventh graders going down the right-hand aisle of the auditorium. They checked in with Mr. Parazzo, who stood by the rows of seats assigned to his homeroom. They each took a copy of the handout he offered. As other students came up, Mikey and Margalo slipped away, to push their way back up to the rear of the room. They would be out the doors long before anybody else, when this assembly disassembled.

Seated, they each opened a big, loose-leaf notebook and impaled the handout on its three rings, as if the paper was a three-hearted Dracula. Each took out a pen and put her initials at the top of the paper. *ME,* wrote Mikey, in large, dark letters. *Me,* Margalo wrote, perhaps more modestly.

"Why do they always schedule assemblies during civics?" Mikey wondered as she looked out over the audience, which was busy talking, checking in, talking, finding seats, talking, looking around to see who was looking around at them.

Margalo had an explanation. "It's because governments prefer their voters uninformed. So, actually, this assembly is a *part* of civics class: We're learning to keep ourselves uninformed." Then she had to admit, "Although it's not just civics. It's every seventh-period class, on Wednesdays."

"You mean some people get to miss English?" Mikey realized, outraged.

"Or gym."

"I *like* gym," Mikey said.

They closed their notebooks. Neither one read the handout.

Onstage, the blue velvet curtain hung closed, but an empty podium waited at center stage. Because this was a class meeting, not an all-school assembly, only half of the auditorium filled up.

Mikey estimated the size of the audience. "About a hundred and ninety?"

"There are two hundred and five people in the class," Margalo answered.

"Minus the usual absentee rate of five percent."

Margalo tried to work that out in her head. Divide by ten, she told herself. Now, divide by two. Now subtract.

Mikey figured it out in about one second. "One hundred ninety-five, probably."

Margalo was slow, but she was accurate. "One hundred ninety-four and three-quarters," she corrected. Then she had to get grinned at and punched in the arm.

Mikey continued. "So what we have here is about a hundred ninety-five twelve- and thirteen-year-old boys and girls, of varius colors and creeds. A perfect slice of the American pie."

Margalo pointed out, "At least one of them is only eleven." This was Hadrian Klenk.

"But he's probably the smartest kid in the whole seventh grade."

"Maybe the whole school, maybe the whole school system, but so what?"

"You mean, since that doesn't make him any less of an unpopular dork?" Mikey asked.

"Although it does make him the smartest unpopular dork."

"That's the clique I belong in, Smart Unpopular Dorks," Mikey said, perfectly happy. "SUDs. You want to be in it? You're smart enough."

"I'm not unpopular," Margalo protested. "Not like you."

They could talk without worrying about being overheard, since the room was loud with conversations and laughter as the rows below them filled up and Mr. Saunders ascended the four steps to the stage.

"So I win again," Mikey said in a lowered voice.

As Mr. Saunders looked out over his audience, he noticed Mikey and Margalo. Actually, "noticed" was too mild a word. His attention fell on them, like the blue laser beam out of the eyes of an alien invader. Mikey and Margalo looked back at him from where they sat alone in the empty rear of the auditorium.

Frowning a little, Mr. Saunders raised his right hand, flipped it up into the air—instructing them to stand up—and pointed to the last filled row, half an auditorium away.

Everybody turned to see what he was looking at. But everybody turned right back, because Mr. Saunders started talking. "Good afternoon, boys and girls," he was saying, as Mikey and Margalo slowly rose from their seats to move up. Mr. Saunders was so tall, he had to lean down a little to get his mouth close enough to the microphone. His voice was so deep and loud that he had to speak softly into the microphone. He told them it was going to be his pleasure to announce the seventh-grade honor roll students, those with B averages. After that, he told them, it would be his pleasure to read them the very short list of high honor roll students, who had straight A's. Then he had one announcement to make, before he came to the real purpose of this assembly, which was the big seventh-grade class project of the year, which was the eighth-grade dance.

As he spoke, he watched Mikey and Margalo sit down, still three rows back from the rest of the students. He watched, but decided not to say anything as he unfolded a sheet of paper.

Mikey said to Margalo, "High honor roll's something I could do," and Margalo whispered back, "Pipe down."

Mr. Saunders read out the forty-six names on the honor roll, in alphabetical order. When he'd finished, he asked those students to stand and receive the applause of their less fortunate—probably because less hard-working—peers. Mikey and Margalo stood up and applauded one another.

Next Mr. Saunders read off the names of the three girls on the high honor roll list, and the one boy. Hadrian Klenk, the only boy with straight A's, bobbed up and sank right back down into his corner seat, in the front row.

Mikey refused to stay piped down. "I'll make high honor roll next marking period."

"We both could," Margalo realized.

"Math," Mikey reminded her.

Mr. Saunders moved on to his next topic, which was the importance of school spirit. He urged all of the seventh graders to come to games, and cheer on the West School teams, just as they hoped to be cheered on next year, when they were the ones playing. "There's nothing like hometown support," Mr. Saunders said,

93

"nothing as important as your friends being behind you as you try your hardest."

"So all I can do this year is sit in the stands?" Mikey asked. "What's wrong with this picture?"

Those two major topics, academics and athletics, covered, Mr. Saunders got down to the purpose of the assembly: the dance. Every year at West Junior High, the seventh grade hosted a dance for the eighth grade. Mr. Saunders devoted a few seconds to brushing aside his audience's initial response to this announcement before instructing them to look at their handouts.

Mikey and Margalo obeyed, opening their notebooks across their laps. Under the cover of that diversion, Margalo insisted, "I could work harder and do better in math; I could try harder. I won't ever understand, but that doesn't mean I can't get an A."

"Hunnh," Mikey answered, wordlessly doubting it.

Mr. Saunders wanted them to read along with him as he read the handout aloud, probably to guarantee that they understood it, but maybe only to be sure this class meeting didn't get out early. The items were:

1. It was a tradition at West Junior High for the seventh grade to give this dance, although—

2. Seventh graders couldn't attend it themselves, unless—

3. They were asked by an eighth grader, as a date.

4. Valentine's Day was the traditional time for the dance.

5. The seventh-grade class would need to raise over one hundred dollars to cover the cost of music, decorations, and refreshments.

6. Committees would be formed to work on these various aspects of the project. Every seventh grader had to serve on a committee.

7. The usual forms of publicity were what was permitted: posters and flyers, a newspaper interview; nothing beyond that without his approval.

8. The seventh grade would have to find at least ten adult chaperones, preferably from the faculty, and—

9. The most important point: Every homeroom, every seventh grader, was responsible to see that the gym—where the dance would be held—was cleaned up afterward, and ready for the first phys ed class on the Monday morning after the dance.

10. These handouts were to be taken home, shown to parents, signed, and returned to their homeroom teachers. By Friday.

During this, Mikey busied herself writing along the margins of the paper *ME, ME, ME,* until her initials began to resemble one of those Greek designs around the water jugs they had seen slides of in seminar.

"Any questions?" Mr. Saunders asked, as if he really wanted to hear some.

Mikey looked up, to show that she was paying attention, which she wasn't; the principal was scanning the audience for raised hands. He didn't want to miss anybody's question, no matter what it was. Even if it was the inevitable give-away question, "Does every seventh grader have to participate?", Mr. Saunders answered it patiently. Even the inevitable giggly question, "If an eighth grade boy asks you"—interrupted by the inevitable sarcastic comment, "In your dreams an eighth-grade boy will ask *you*"—didn't shake his calm.

Margalo was busy looking over the audience, noticing how—with Mr. Saunders ready to pounce on them—the boys were neither punching shoulders nor elbowing, but were still visibly restless. The girls had their heads bent over the handout papers, sitting still, whispering without looking like they were. "Why do they make the seventh grade give a dance?" Margalo asked Mikey.

"Because nobody wants to?" Mikey guessed.

They spoke in low voices, stiff-lipped like ventriloquists, and kept their eyes on their handouts, as if they were reading them carefully.

Margalo rephrased her question. "It's eighth graders who always talk about dances, and dates. They're the ones who should give a dance."

"Eighth grade does sound pretty bad," Mikey agreed. "Except, I'll get to play on the tennis team."

"Their class project is a play. But none of *them* want to do *that*, either. It's so perfectly backwards from what the students want to do, it has to be on purpose, don't you think?" Margalo asked.

Mikey shook her head, denying it. "They don't know enough about us to do it on purpose." Then she smiled—lots of teeth, *Who me? Little-old-me?*—at Mr. Saunders, whose attention had been attracted by her shaking head.

Mr. Saunders smiled back. *Good-girls.*

Mikey kept on smiling.

His expression grew wary. His smile changed. *I've-got-my-eye-on-you*, he smiled and went back to his agenda.

"In your committees, you will first estimate your expenses and then consider ways of raising the necessary funds. This two-step process is a good rule to follow for all of life," he advised them.

That wasn't bad advice, in Mikey's opinion. Pay your own way. She agreed one hundred percent about that. She figured, if you were paying your own way, you could go wherever you wanted.

"In our experience," Mr. Saunders told his audience, "it will cost you at least one hundred and twenty-five dollars to put on a successful dance."

A few moans and whistles and complaints accompanied this information. "Too muches" bounced around off of "Not enoughs," like little boats on a sea of "Who cares-es?"

"Other seventh-grade classes have done it," Mr. Saunders told them. "Do you think you can't do as well as all the other seventh-grade classes who have been at West Junior High? I know better than that," he reassured them. He offered the bribe of his esteem. "In fact, I wouldn't be surprised if your class didn't give the best dance ever."

His confidence raised their interest.

"So let's brainstorm about how to raise money," he exhorted, like a politician urging people to vote for him, or a general getting his troops eager to march off and die. "Let's just get started and do it. Yes, Louis?"

"A boxing match," Louis Caselli suggested. He hadn't changed since the first time Mikey and Margalo had laid eyes on him, in fifth grade. It was almost fun, how predictable Louis Caselli was, when it wasn't totally boring. "People would pay to see that."

Mr. Saunders had a yellow pad out, and a pen in his hand, but he wasn't writing this down. "That's not exactly—"

"Or wrestling," Louis suggested. "Or karate, like *The Karate Kid,*" Louis concluded, speaking loudly now so Mr. Saunders could hear him over the enthusiastic support of those boys who thought this was one great idea.

Mr. Saunders raised his voice two notches. "That's enough, boys." As if a wet blanket had been thrown down over them, the boys settled down.

"The guy is good at his job," Mikey said. "I have to give him that."

They went through the predictable suggestions, which Mr. Saunders did write down—car washes, bake sales, bottle drives. There were also some more self-interested ones, like Rhonda's suggestion of a fashion show. "With a lunch. We could set out tables in the gym and—we could see if the department stores in the mall will sponsor us. The girls who were

99

models would all be seventh graders," she promised.

"What about boys?"

"Boy models?"

"Do you think you're *that* good-looking?"

A Heather suggested, "Boys could be the waiters."

"What about a fair?" a Lindsay suggested. "We did that in my old school, every March. We got our computers with the money we made; we made a lot."

"My mom could teach dance, ballroom, disco, line dancing. She knows them all."

"How about a touch football tournament?" Louis asked, without being called on. He'd been waving his hand around for a while without attracting Mr. Saunders's attention.

Mikey was groaning softly. "Bo-ring," she chanted. "Bo-ring, -ring, -ring," and Margalo didn't argue. She looked at Mikey and grinned. They chanted softly in unison, "Bo-ring, -ring, -ring."

Louis continued explaining his idea as Mr. Saunders, carrying the microphone in one hand, its cord trailing behind like a giant, skinny possum tail, or a giant, skinny umbilical cord, came down to ground level. "See, we could charge an entry fee, for each team to play. All the guys would like it."

"What about the girls?" a girl demanded.

"Girls could have baking contests. Or sewing contests." Mr. Saunders didn't stop him and Louis was feeling smart, feeling important. "Or, girls could sell kisses."

Groans mingled with "*All-rights*," while clumps of girls made flurrying flattered noises.

"I'm never going to make it through two years," Mikey moaned.

"High school won't be any better," Margalo warned her.

"We'll be older," Mikey said, without enthusiasm. "We can get jobs, and work," she pointed out. Then she got very quiet.

This was not because Mr. Saunders was coming up the aisle toward them, spreading silence out behind him like a supertanker spreading its huge wake. The approach of Mr. Saunders was why Margalo got quiet, but not Mikey. Mikey had her own reasons.

Before he came to the end of the filled rows, Mr. Saunders stopped, facing them.

Margalo pretended to be riveted to something that was going on, onstage. She raised her hand and waved it frantically in the air, *Call on me, please, call on me.*

Satisfied, Mr. Saunders turned around.

But Mikey had gotten quiet because her brain had

gone into gear. It shifted into first and then sped right up to fifth, and the words burst out of her. "What if—"

"Shhsh," Margalo whispered and waved her hand in the direction of Mr. Saunders's back.

The principal turned around again, but Mikey still hadn't noticed him.

"No, it's a great idea—what if I'm a millionaire before I'm twenty?"

Margalo pretended she was deaf, and interested only in the handout on her lap, and totally alone in the row, sitting next to someone she'd never seen before.

Mr. Saunders came to stand right beside Mikey. He didn't say a word.

Mikey looked up at him and lowered her voice to a stage whisper. "Tell you later," she said to Margalo, who was pretending to be invisible. Then Mikey looked up at Mr. Saunders, who loomed above her, the microphone in his hand, and stage whispered, *"Zut, alors!"*

8
What If-?

"I'm not going to let them get away with this," Mikey told Margalo. "I have a plan."

"I know," Margalo said, not particularly interested in being ranted at.

They were jouncing along home on the school bus. Mikey sat by the window, but she wasn't looking out of it. Nobody paid any attention to them, and they didn't pay attention to anybody else; at least, Mikey didn't.

"Okay, Miss I Already Know Everything, what *is* my plan?" Mikey asked.

"To make a million dollars," Margalo said, then she remembered, "unless it's to make high honor roll."

"Wrong twice," Mikey answered, then she corrected herself, "wrong once, because I *am* going to get on the high honor roll. But this is the real plan: I'm going to play on the West tennis team in the spring."

Sometimes, Margalo thought Mikey must spend her waking hours figuring out ways to make herself even more unpopular.

Mikey explained, "They'll keep me off the team just because I'm not in eighth grade and that stinks. I mean, it really *stinks*."

"You'll be in eighth grade next year. You'll get your turn."

"Also, it's hypocritical," Mikey said. "Because they assign us to classes by ability. Like, the seminars are only for the best students, and the way they do the sectioning for college prep classes. And like even *having* college prep classes in seventh grade."

"They won't change the policy," Margalo predicted.

"You don't get it. I'm right. They're wrong. It's going to be easy."

"I don't *think* so," Margalo said. "Although . . ." She was having the beginning of an idea, herself.

"Besides, it'll give me something to do," Mikey argued. "Look at our lives, Margalo. We sit in class, we learn what they tell us to, we go home and do homework. I *ask* you," she told Margalo.

"School's not all that simple for me," Margalo pointed out. She had to figure out which teachers preferred you to repeat back their own opinions and which wanted you to contradict them; which wanted you to ask questions and which preferred sponges for students. She needed to learn to predict the kinds of questions she was going to get on tests and what kinds of answers would get her the best grades. Not to mention tracking the interests and opinions of the other students, itself a full-time job. "I'm not bored at school," she said.

"You should be," Mikey announced. "Besides, you know it's not fair if I can't play on the team just because I'm a seventh grader."

Even if she agreed, Margalo didn't want to hear any more about this. In fact, she didn't care much about it. In fact, if somebody asked her about what was boring, she would probably answer: getting bent out of shape because seventh graders couldn't play on school teams.

That, however, she didn't tell Mikey. Instead, she asked, "What dumb committee do we want to be on for the dumb dance?"

"None," Mikey said.

"Yeah. But every seventh grader has to."

"And that's not fair, either," Mikey said.

Sometimes, Margalo thought, Mikey was more trouble than she was worth.

"I'm going to make an appointment with Mr. Saunders," was how Mikey greeted her the next morning. Not, "Good luck on the math quiz," but only her *own* hot news.

Even if Margalo *had* been thinking about this team situation, she still wanted a best friend who didn't think exclusively about herself. So Margalo was grumpy, and Mikey decided, "I guess you're going to start your period. About time. Do you have extra zits this week?"

Maybe that was Mikey's idea of best friendship. Sometimes it wasn't Margalo's, so she was glad to spend most of that morning not in Mikey's company. Although the idea of starting her period—because it *was* about time—cheered her up.

On a whim, the cheered-up Margalo stopped by Ronnie Caselli's desk before English class started and said, "Hey." She could see that Ronnie was glad she did.

That told Margalo that Ronnie was sorry for the way she'd treated Mikey, about the dinner party and afterward, too. Ronnie would probably never say it—she was a Caselli, after all, and Mikey was Mikey—but she wouldn't do it again, either.

"Hihowareyou?" Ronnie smiled, a big smile. "You're looking good—but you always do."

Margalo kept the compliments even. "I like those barrettes." Ronnie held her hair back from her face with three barrettes, two on one side, one on the other, all of them looking like tiny glass daisies in pale tones of pink and blue and purple.

"I got them this weekend, at the mall."

"Expensive?" Margalo asked, as if she could even think of buying herself fancy hair barrettes.

"Not too bad. I've been doing a lot of baby-sitting."

"I wish I could baby-sit for money." Margalo meant it, but she also meant to flatter. Who doesn't like to be told she's more fortunate than you?

A few girls entered the class. "Hey, Ronnie," they said and, seeing Margalo, "Hey, Margalo." "Hey," and "Hihowareyou," Margalo and Ronnie answered.

"You know what I wish?" Ronnie said then, looking up at Margalo, who was still loitering near her desk. "No, really, I really do. I wish Mikey wasn't so immature. Don't you? Because she's okay, in lots of ways, except—she's so immature," Ronnie repeated. And suddenly Margalo didn't care very much at all if Mikey *was* so self-centered. "She gets everybody angry," Ronnie said. "I can't tell—do you think she does it on purpose? She's really lucky you stick with her, isn't she?"

Later, Margalo wished she had said something instead of mouthing vague sounds, "ummble, bluughgle," to avoid saying anything. But she hadn't, and the real reason she hadn't was because she didn't want Ronnie to know she disagreed; and she knew that about herself, even while she was ummble-bluughgleing away. She knew it and she didn't much like it.

One of the things Margalo liked best about Mikey, she decided, was the way Mikey never kept her mouth shut when she had an opinion.

So that by the time they sat down together in the cafeteria, Margalo was glad to have Mikey for a best friend, and ready to talk about the school team question. "Going to Mr. Saunders isn't the first thing to do," she told Mikey.

"Who asked you?" Mikey was looking at her plate: chicken à la king served over an ice-cream scoop of rice, with a serving of limp, skinny green beans lying on their sides. "Where's Heather when I really need her?" Mikey groused, then asked, "Can green beans have anorexia?"

Margalo explained, "They're french cut."

"That was a joke, Dumby."

"That was a joke?" Margalo asked. *Dumby?*"

A reluctant laugh escaped from Mikey's control.

Margalo unwrapped her sandwich, packaged boiled ham on supermarket rye bread, with mustard and a slice of American cheese.

"So instead of going straight to Mr. Saunders, you think I'd be smarter to start with Miss Sanabria?" Mikey asked. Miss Sanabria was one of the four girls' gym teachers; she also coached the seventh-grade basketball players and was assistant coach to the eighth-grade girls' team. When Margalo nodded, a slow *Maybe* nod, Mikey said, "That's good thinking." Which was about as close to "thank you" as Mikey ever got.

"Actually," Margalo said, "I think that you should reconsider the whole plan."

And Mikey interrupted. "You always try to fix up my ideas."

"You always go in swinging," Margalo pointed out.

They were quiet for a minute. Margalo waited to be asked how she would do it. Mikey wasn't about to ask her anything.

"The thing is," Mikey said, "you always make things so complicated."

"Things *are* complicated."

"Not always. And I might go in swinging, but at least I connect." Then Mikey added, to be honest, "Most of the time."

"Okay," Margalo admitted. "But here you're talking about asking the principal to change school policy. You're talking about teachers, adults. Things are always more complicated when adults get involved."

"Still—" Mikey started to say.

Margalo cut her off, passing over one of the two sugared chocolate doughnuts she'd put in that morning, even though personally she didn't like to have so much sugar so close to her teeth.

Mikey stopped talking to chomp down on the doughnut, which gave Margalo time to suggest, "You should talk to some of the seventh graders first, maybe get them to sign a petition. Then you could have a groundswell of popular opinion behind you when you go to ask Mr. Saunders about it. That would put you in a stronger negotiating position."

By the time Mikey swallowed, and washed the doughnut down with milk, she had seen Margalo's point. "I've got until spring, so there's time. How many signatures would make a good petition? Would coaches sign, do you think? Would you ask them? And teachers?"

"Actually, I was thinking," Margalo suggested, "what if you went out for basketball?"

"Why would I do *that?*"

"Because winter is basketball season," Margalo explained. "So instead of waiting for the spring tennis season, you could go out for basketball. You could agitate to get seventh graders on the girls' basketball team. Because, here's what I think," she said, but instead of speaking she reached into her brown bag and took out an orange. She made the first break in its skin with her teeth, then started peeling it with her fingers, carefully putting all the peels in a pile she could move back into her brown paper bag.

Mikey watched this, waiting, for about two seconds. "I'll agitate *you*," she muttered. "Spit it out, Margalo. I know you've got some whole plan worked out."

"Okay." Margalo took a breath. "I think you should make a big fuss about seventh graders being on the basketball team, and get people to sign a petition for that, and then give in gracefully when Mr. Saunders says no. Then, when you come back to ask about playing on the tennis team, he'll say yes."

Mikey didn't see it. "If he won't in January, why would he in March?"

"Because they want to say yes to students, but they never like to make exceptions. They want to be popular, well-liked—stern and well-liked, that's a teacher's dream. But they're afraid of looking weak. They'll take the easiest way, which is usually the way of no-change. But if it's just you, and just tennis— which is played one-on-one—"

"Doubles isn't."

"You know what I mean. Tennis isn't like a team sport; there aren't a lot of players involved. I think if you've already softened them up over basketball, then I bet they'll let you play tennis. If you really are good enough," Margalo concluded, deliberately provoking.

"I'm good enough," Mikey said. "More than good enough."

"Anyway, that's my plan."

"I'm a natural athlete." Mikey returned to the chicken à la king, which she had stirred into the rice. "I'll probably even be a pretty good basketball player. Dad and I watch it a lot on TV, so I know the game.

Getting good enough will give me something to do, so that's another advantage. *You* can go around talking to people about how unfair it is, and getting them to sign a petition. We don't have much time, Margalo," she said urgently.

"Much time for what?" Frannie Arenberg asked, sitting down beside Margalo. "What are those red things in the stew, Mikey?" she asked. "Are you going to eat them?"

"Time for getting a petition signed, to let seventh-grade girls play on the basketball team," Margalo said, but Mikey answered, "Pimentos. They're supposed to add flavor. Haven't you ever had creamed chicken?"

Frannie shook her head. "My father does the cooking. Which committee are you going to be on? Because I think you should be on the bake sale. Everyone says Mrs. Draper had to admit you did the best baking, even if she didn't like your attitude."

"I'm a pretty good cook," Mikey said, and Margalo said the same thing at the same time. "She's a good cook." Then Margalo turned to Mikey and said, "We have to be on some committee."

"I will if you will," Mikey said. "It'll just be baking stuff at home and bringing it in to sell. I can teach you stuff," she pointed out.

Margalo wasn't sure she wanted to be Mikey's student.

"You'll learn how to make my mother's chocolate chip cookies," Mikey offered.

Margalo considered that. There was no other committee she wanted to be on, so she agreed. "Okay. What about you?" she asked Frannie.

"They asked me to be on publicity. We're going to design our stuff on the school computers, and they're making that little computer whiz be on the committee, too. Hadrian."

Margalo said, "Actually, Hadrian's young, not little. Because he skipped two grades."

"He's still shorter than anybody else," Frannie pointed out. "But if he skipped and he's young, why do they tease him?"

"You aren't asking that seriously, are you?" Mikey wondered, adding, "While we're on the subject of short, do you play basketball?"

9

Can Unpopular People Have a Popular Opinion?

*B*etween the bake sale committee and the basketball petition, Margalo thought she'd prefer the committee, but she was wrong. It turned out that on the committee, Mikey tried to run things and—big surprise—nobody wanted her to.

"She's not the boss," people protested to Margalo when Mikey told them what to bake. "Who died and made her queen of the world?" they groused when she told them to have the first bake sale in early December. "What makes her think I even care if she likes my recipe?"

Because the bake sale committee was the largest, they met in the library during assembly period. They pushed tables together to make one big table. Mrs. Draper, the home economics teacher, was their faculty adviser. Except that every single person on the committee was female; they were a diverse group. There were a few preppies and several jockettes, as well as two girls from the arty-smarty clique. There were two Barbies, both brunettes, and about six of the not popular and unpopular girls, including Mikey and Margalo. Everybody had recipe ideas, except Margalo, and everybody wanted to have names put beside the platters to say who baked them, except Mikey, and everybody wanted a chance to sit at the bake sale table and sell, except Mikey and Margalo.

Mrs. Draper kept lists and overruled ideas. "Cookies, brownies, and bars," she suggested.

Her committee, hands raised and waving, like baby birds in a nest squeaking for their mother to drop worms into their mouths, insisted on suggesting cakes and pies that absolutely everybody always loved.

Mrs. Draper vetoed briskly. "Too hard to serve. Too messy to eat."

One of the Barbies had a Greek mother who knew how to make baklava, which Mrs. Draper vetoed as "too sticky," and one of the jockettes had a recipe for penuche, which Mrs. Draper shook her head at. "Too strange."

Mikey had been thinking. "Cupcakes," she announced, without raising her hand. Mrs. Draper had to write that down because cupcakes were easy to serve. Mikey followed up her advantage. "Tarts."

Mrs. Draper wrote that down, too, then said, "That's enough out of you for a while, Mikey."

Once they had decided on what they would bake, and that the bake sales would commence on the first Friday after Thanksgiving vacation, they had to decide how much to charge.

Mikey was all for the highest possible prices. "*My* cookies are worth what you pay for those cookies at the mall, and those aren't half as good. I can promise you that." Most of the other committee members believed that charging less would sell more and thus earn them more.

"That's only in the short run," Mikey argued. "Because if people think they're getting more for their money, they'll pay more and they'll buy just as many."

"I think we'd better vote on this," Mrs. Draper suggested.

"Then charge more just for mine," Mikey suggested.

"We'll do what the majority wants, Mikey," Mrs. Draper decided.

Margalo admired the way Mrs. Draper could be authoritative when she needed to be, but democratic when the vote was sure to come out the way she wanted. Everybody said how fair their adviser was, and how she treated them like they were grown-up. Everybody except Margalo, who didn't think it was nearly as simple as that, and Mikey, who didn't get what she wanted nearly often enough on Mrs. Draper's committee.

"All I'm going to be doing is baking, anyway, so rats on the rest of it," Mikey announced.

"As if we care," the committee responded.

Work on the petition went more placidly, probably because it was only Mikey and Margalo doing it. It went without saying that it would be a bad idea for Mikey to try to get signatures, and a disaster for Margalo to try to play basketball. So on Sunday afternoon, while Margalo entered into Mr. Elsinger's computer the petition they had composed, Mikey practiced by playing one-on-one against her father. She didn't cut him any slack.

Margalo printed out four copies of the petition and considered how to go about collecting signatures.

The way she figured it was this: A real drawback to not being popular was people don't want to agree with you. So if you're not popular and you're asking people to sign a petition, you have to do it the right way.

Unfortunately, as Margalo knew, one reason a person isn't popular is because for some mysterious reason she doesn't do things the right way. She probably doesn't know what the right way even is, and maybe doesn't even know there *is* a right way. Margalo wasn't exactly in that position, but she was close enough so that if she went about getting signatures the wrong way, she could easily turn herself from a not-particularly-popular person into a positively un-popular one, *and* not get any signatures.

Which would about shut down her social life entirely, since Mikey would be furious at her.

So Margalo would have to be smart about how she asked for signatures.

Her most interesting idea, as she thought about this problem, was: People think there's only one right way to do anything, a secret right way known only to the special people who belong to the Secret Right Way Knowing Club, but there are a lot of different right ways—and also a lot of different wrong ways.

This was interesting. Margalo was having a good time, no question. She reread the petition:

To the faculty and administration of West Junior High School: We protest your policy of excluding seventh-grade girls from the basketball team. Seventh graders would benefit from the on-court experience of games with eighth graders. Also, practices are held after school hours, and any player who couldn't keep her grades up would be dropped from the squad, so there is no good reason for the policy. We believe it isn't fair to not let us play.

Below that statement were numbered places for signatures, in two columns, fifteen in each column.

Margalo was guessing that only the principal could change policy. He was the one she was really firing her cannon at. She didn't plan to win this battle, but she did plan to do enough damage, so that their next attack—the tennis attack—would be against a weakened and wounded enemy, a Mr. Saunders who would probably just as soon have a player as good as Mikey play on the West tennis team anyway.

It could all work out, Margalo thought. She could make it all work out.

Margalo began Monday morning, in English, with Ronnie Caselli and the preppies. Actually, she began earlier on Monday, when she dressed for school. Her dress style for approaching the preppies was the Old Boyfriend look, which meant she had to wait until her stepbrother left for school so she could raid his closet and take out his tweed jacket, the one good jacket he owned. She put it on over her outfit (mid-calf black skirt, jewel-necked peach sweater) and folded back the sleeves. Howie wasn't that much taller than she was—well, who was?—but his shoulders were broader, so the jacket hung off her just the way it was supposed to.

She knew how to greet Ronnie, like giving the secret password signal that gets you into the clubhouse. "Hihowareyou?"

"Cool," Ronnie answered. "Great jacket."

Margalo told the truth. Sometimes, the truth was a better story than anything she could make up. "I borrowed it from Howie. *After* he left the house."

"I know what you mean," Ronnie said. "My brothers would kill me—and my mother would, too."

"Aurora believes in nonviolence," Margalo answered, and Ronnie laughed. "I wish *my* mother did."

People were entering the classroom, settling into their usual seats. Margalo took out her notebook and opened it to show Ronnie the petition. "Tell me what you think of this."

Surprised, Ronnie read it quickly, then looked around to see who might give her a second opinion. This was just what Margalo had expected, which was why she had chosen English class, where Heather McGinty wasn't. Annie Piers, Heather McGinty's henchperson and chief rival, *was* in the class, however, and Ronnie called her over.

"Hihowareyou," Margalo greeted Annie.

"Cool," Annie answered, and her eyes lingered on the jacket. "How about you, Ron?" she asked, and Ronnie answered, "Cool, how about you?" and Annie said coolly, "As you see."

Then Ronnie asked her, "What do you think of this?"

While Annie bent over the desk to read, Ronnie asked Margalo just the two questions Margalo expected. First she asked, "What's gotten you interested in sports?"

Margalo could be as cool as they were, and cooler. "Take a look at the signatures."

There were only two signatures, and number one was Mikey Elsinger.

"Is Mikey going out for basketball?" Ronnie asked.

"What do you think?" Margalo asked back.

"I can dig it," Ronnie said.

"I don't know," Annie Piers said, now, talking to Ronnie, ignoring Margalo. "Are you going to sign it?"

"Well, when we were in fifth grade and there was a boys' only soccer team, Mikey—"

The teacher entered, and everyone scurried to a desk. "Tell you after," Ronnie called softly to Annie's back, and to Margalo, who was gathering up her notebook, she asked just what Margalo hoped to hear. "See you at lunch?"

Ronnie didn't mean at lunch, exactly, not lunch at her table. She meant "at lunchtime, in the hallway, by my locker." So Margalo wasn't surprised to see Ronnie and Annie and Heather McGinty, too, with a couple of the Aceys and another Heather, all gathered together, by the seventh-grade lockers, at the start of first lunch.

"What's this petition?" Heather McGinty asked, and Margalo showed it to her. Heather read it and was about to say No Way, Nix, Nothing Doing, when Margalo spoke.

"I wanted to ask you people first," she said, talking to Ronnie. "Because it would be so cool to get the rule changed, you know? Student power and all that. Ronnie knows about Mikey," Margalo said, looking around at all of them, looking right into Heather McGinty's catlike face with its greeny eyes and little chin. "Mikey makes things happen. Like in fifth grade, remember?" she asked Ronnie.

"What you were telling me," Annie said to Ronnie.

"I don't know," Heather McGinty said, doubt in her voice. "I don't—"

Margalo pounced, pretending that Heather was about to say what she knew perfectly well Heather hadn't even thought of. "I know it's hard to believe that students can change school policy, but sometimes, if the right students go about it the right way, they can really do it. And make a big difference to all the rest of us," Margalo said, speaking to Annie now, and the Aceys, and the other Heather.

"That's true," Ronnie said. "We never thought Mikey'd get girls on the soccer team in fifth grade. But she did."

"That was Mikey?" asked one of the Aceys, Casey Wolsowski. "You guys went to Washington?"

Margalo nodded.

Casey turned her beady brown eyes on Heather McGinty to ask, "What do you have against signing?"

Annie Piers sensed a leadable opposition and rushed forward. "Yeah, Heather. It sounds sort of cool to me."

"Don't sign if you don't want to," Margalo said now. "I'm not going to give up, we aren't, so don't worry about that. It would just—oh, you know, be easier if you people agreed with us, and everyone could see that you did—but—" She reached out to take the paper back.

Ronnie protested, "I didn't say I didn't want to sign."

"I'll sign," Annie said, and signed. "Casey?" Casey signed. "Ronnie? Stacey, Heather, anybody else? C'mon, Heather," she nudged Heather McGinty with an elbow. "Everybody's forgotten your little feud with Mikey," she reminded everyone. "So you should, too. Besides, this has nothing to do with that. This is for all of us."

There was no way Heather McGinty could not sign, then, and everybody else followed her example, which gave Margalo seven signatures, now. "Thanks," she said, when the last pen was put away.

"I'd love a chance to play on the school basketball

team," Ronnie said. "I'll go to basketball practice, anyway, but it would be more fun if I had a chance to make the team. Are you playing basketball, Annie?"

"Where'd you get that jacket?" Annie Piers finally gave in and asked it, so Margalo told her, "Around the house. I've got all these older stepbrothers," she added with a cool, careless shrug, before she went off to join Mikey for lunch.

Mikey wasn't interested in anything but the question of how well she would do in her first basketball practice, and whether Margalo would take the late bus with her today, or go home early.

"Early. I didn't tell Aurora we'd be on the late bus, so she'd worry."

"Call her," Mikey suggested, but Margalo shook her head. She wasn't wasting any quarter of hers on a pay phone. "You'll have to wait for hours to hear how it goes," Mikey argued.

"I think I can stand that." Also, Margalo needed to get this jacket back into Howard's closet before he arrived home from school.

"But what about me having to stand the wait to tell you?" Mikey demanded, chomping down on a slice of pizza, not even offering Margalo a bite.

"Where's your petition?" Frannie asked, setting

her tray down on their table, asking Margalo, "Want a slice? Their pizza's pretty good." So Margalo took just the triangular tip of a slice while Frannie signed the petition and offered to help get more signatures. "We can wait outside the library, one on each side of the doors, in the morning before school starts," she suggested to Margalo, who hadn't even *hoped* for something as perfect as Frannie Arenberg wanting to help out.

On Tuesday, Margalo wore one of her stepsister Susannah's old polos (for which she traded a night's dishwashing) and jeans for once; she wore her gym sneakers, because even if they weren't regulation Reeboks or Nikes, sneakers were still athletic shoes. She sat down at Tanisha's table at lunch—not to unpack her sandwich and eat, just to greet Tanisha and everybody else there, a long table of jockettes, "Hey, Tan, hey, everybody. Whazzup?"

"Whazzup?" they asked her back, and she told them. They signed the petition enthusiastically.

Wednesday, Margalo wore black over black. She drifted into the art studio before morning homeroom. She'd left Frannie sitting at a table in the library, reading the *Monitor* to find current events topics for civics, with a copy of the petition beside her in case anybody wanted to come up and sign. Frannie didn't pick out targets and talk them into it; she just sat there and the targets came humming up to her, like bees to a flower.

Margalo preferred moving around, getting people to want to do what she wanted them to want to do.

In the art studio, nobody noticed her entry. Students, both boys and girls, both seventh graders and eighth, drooped beside the windows in boredom and drooped over desks in anticipation of more boredom to come; three were talking intently about a painting set out on an easel. Margalo approached a group of girls. One of them—Cassie—was in her math class. All looked curiously at her. "Hey, Cassie, what's new?" Margalo said.

"What ever is?" Cassie answered. "You guys know Margalo?"

They shook their heads, no, they didn't know her, but, "Like the skirt," one of them said.

"We're in the same math," Cassie explained to her friends, and, "I'm more impressive in English," Margalo explained to Cassie.

"Hey, that's not a criticism," Cassie said. "There

should always be a couple of us who just don't get it, in every class. It lowers the teacher's expectations."

"But I'm not *playing* dumb," Margalo said, and Cassie laughed. "Do you guys want to sign a petition?" Margalo asked then. She had decided that it would be stupid to try to conceal or misrepresent the petition's nature from these girls. They were the arty-smarty clique; maybe not top students, but no dummies. "Any of you? Because we're trying to get the policy about seventh-grade girls not being allowed to play on the basketball team changed. Because it's not at all fair and it's maybe even discriminatory," she explained.

"That's sports," one of the girls said, but another took the bait. "Discriminatory?"

"Yeah," Margalo said. "You know, though, what really puzzles me? Why the boys haven't tried to do anything about it. Oh, well. Maybe they're too busy worrying about winning. Anyway, do any of you want to look at the petition?"

They did, and three of them wanted to sign, and they all knew other people who would probably be interested. "So, where are copies of these things posted?" they asked.

"I have one, and Frannie Arenberg has one. We're usually in the library after lunch," Margalo said.

Cassie responded, "Frannie's always helping out, isn't she?" and one of the group added, "Next time you want to do a petition, or anything like that, you ought to talk to me. The layout of this really sucks."

By Wednesday lunch, both Margalo and Frannie were on their third petition pages, and things had slowed down a little. In the cafeteria, Margalo saw Frannie sitting at a table with Heather James and Annie Piers, Heather McGinty and Casey Wolsowski; and she watched Louis Caselli approach them. He was wearing a green, roll-neck J.Crew sweater, trying for a preppy look. He tapped Frannie on the shoulder and said something to her. She smiled up at him, then reached down to her pile of books to take out the petition. Louis took it from her and stood there, at her shoulder, reading it.

He read for a long time.

He was a slow reader, Margalo thought, but not that slow.

Frannie just went back to talking with her friends.

Then Louis tapped her on the shoulder again, and asked her something else. Frannie shook her head and said something, at which Louis looked over to where Margalo was watching.

He tried to argue with Frannie, but Frannie just smiled and shook her head. He gave her back the petition, without signing, and headed for Margalo.

Margalo nudged Mikey, who was eating the pale brown hamburger as if it actually had a taste. "Look who's here," Margalo said. Mikey grunted.

Louis timed the beginning of what he planned to say to match his last step toward their table. But the moment he opened his mouth to speak, Mikey chomped a big bite of her hamburger, and Margalo said, "Nice sweater."

Louis looked confused, briefly, then muttered, "Thanks," to Margalo. He tried to talk to Mikey. "I read—"

Mikey held up a french fry, streaming with catsup. "Want one?"

Louis stepped back as if she had pulled a knife on him, a limp and bloody knife. "This petition," he said, and now he sounded angry, which was more like him.

"What about it?" Margalo asked. "Nobody's asking you to sign," she added, because Louis was more fun when he was on the defensive.

"Yeah, well, maybe I won't. Since it's all about girls."

"So it's nothing to do with you," Mikey said. "So what do you want, Louis?"

"Nothing." The word was out of his mouth before any thought had entered his brain. He turned away. Then he had to stop, and turn back around, and approach them again, strutting along, as if this was exactly what he'd planned. "If you hadn't left us out of it, I could talk a lot of the guys into signing this."

"I don't know," Margalo said. "The boys' program is the high profile one. If we ask for both, see, we might have less chance of getting what we want for ourselves."

Louis thought hard. "You'd have more signatures," he argued.

"I don't know," Margalo said again.

"I could borrow Frannie's copy," Louis offered, "and ask the guys, ask around. I bet I could get you a lot of signatures, if it was for our team, too."

"It's not fair to leave the boys out," Margalo allowed. "Do you care, Mikey?"

Louis waited.

Mikey took her time. She rubbed at her temples with her fingers. She shrugged, and popped three fries into her mouth. She chewed. When she'd swallowed, she said to Margalo, "I guess, if he wants to."

Margalo was doubtful now. "Are you sure, Mikey?"

Louis lost it. "She just said so, didn't she? Miss Interfering Epps."

Margalo didn't say anything, just stared up at him.

"*What?*" Louis demanded, after a while. "*What?*"

Margalo sighed, a *Too boring for words* sigh. "I guess you can tell Frannie we said it's okay to change 'girls' to 'students' and 'her' to 'their.' Have you got that?" Margalo asked, going back to her bologna sandwich. "Go tell her now."

"But don't try anything funny," Mikey warned him. "No fake signatures or stuff like that. It's Frannie's copy, so she'd get in trouble, and besides, Frannie hates cheaters," she concluded with a big *Would-I-rag-on-you?* smile.

Louis turned pink. He got away, fast.

Mikey finished her hamburger. "That was fun. Did you think he'd?"—and she realized—"you already knew what the changes had to be. You *knew* the boys would ask."

"I thought probably."

"Oddzooks," said Mikey admiringly.

"So, do you want to ask Mrs. Sanabria tomorrow?"

"Are you're sure she'll go along?"

"*Crikey*, Mikey, what do you think I am, a mind

reader? I have no idea if she will. Nothing any teacher did would surprise me."

As if they had heard her and wanted to prove her wrong, the very next day, teachers surprised Margalo twice. First, Margalo was surprised to hear that Mrs. Sanabria had yelled at Mikey for asking her to sign the petition. "She got really griped," Mikey reported, not unhappily. "She made me sit out the whole gym class and told me to think about—and I quote here, Margalo—'Think about other people, for once.' I had to think about more than my own desire to be on a team. She wanted me to think about the eighth grader whose place I'd take away. So, see? Mrs. Sanabria agrees that I'm a natural athlete," Mikey concluded as they met up by the lockers at midmorning.

"Nobody said you aren't," Margalo pointed out. "So I don't know what you're boasting about."

"I'm not boasting. It's a fact."

The second teacher-induced surprise was a speech from mild-mannered Mr. Cohen, in civics, about Henry Thoreau, and civil disobedience, and the weekly dance-planning assemblies, which always preempted his class. Margalo had figured that the teachers were as eager as students to miss classes as often as possible, but not Mr. Cohen, it turned out. He was going on strike, he told them. He was protesting all of the missed classes, which were making it impossible for this section to keep up with the others. He was protesting the only way he knew how, which was to refuse to teach.

Mikey's hand shot up, and she asked him, "How can refusing to teach be a protest against not being allowed to teach?"

"Why don't you go stand in the hall, and see if you can't work that out for yourself," Mr. Cohen shot right back, in a not at all mild-mannered way.

This was not like him. It was much more like him to add, as he did before Mikey had gotten out of the room, "Be sure to get the homework assignment from someone. For when I'm not here."

Later, Margalo asked Mikey what had happened, "when you were exiled from civics."

"Nothing," Mikey said. "It was even more boring than class. Except Mr. Saunders came by. Striding." She mimicked the principal's way of walking the hallways of his school. "Striding, striding, *I'm so important*, you know, the way he does. He sort of glanced at me sideways. Didn't stop. Probably, he figured he

135

already knew what I was in trouble for. Talking in class, because I'm a girl," Mikey explained, although Margalo hadn't asked. "Do you think my petition is ruining his day? Or maybe it's Mr. Cohen's rebellion. Or maybe it's both, maybe both are ganging up together to make Mr. Saunders's life a misery," she said happily.

10

Lose Some, Win Some

"You *have* to come with me," Mikey told Margalo. "It's all your idea."

"Is not," Margalo argued. "Do not."

"Yeah, but you made the plan different from how I was going to do it."

Margalo agreed. "Made it better."

Mikey wanted to argue about that. Margalo could tell. But Mikey also wanted Margalo to go to Mr. Saunders's office with her, to co-present the petition and co-argue in its favor.

"My appointment's at the end of first lunch tomorrow," Mikey told Margalo.

Then Mikey opened her mouth and instead of letting words out she put food in, a forkful of lasagne.

When she tasted it, she swallowed quickly and asked, "You want to trade?"

But Margalo was happy with her egg salad sandwich. Her anti-sog experiment of toasting the bread had proved successful. She just ate on, and didn't say anything.

So when Frannie put her tray down on the table beside Margalo, and pulled out the chair to sit, one-track-mind Mikey started right in. "Don't you think that Margalo should come with me to present the petition to Mr. Saunders?"

"*I'll* go with you, Mikey," Frannie answered. "Come with us," Frannie urged Margalo.

"Okay," Margalo said, because Frannie was the kind of person you wanted to say yes to.

"When is this?" Frannie asked.

But before Mikey could tell her, Tanisha slipped into a chair to ask, "What did Saunders say?"

"I haven't talked to him yet," Mikey answered her.

"He probably already knows about the petition," Tan remarked. She reached over to take a piece of lettuce from Frannie's salad—"Okay, Fran?"—and eat it like a potato chip, bite after bite. "They always know everything. D'you think they have spies?"

"I think they have friends among the students," Frannie said.

"Teachers can't be friends with students," Margalo pointed out.

"They're the boss," Mikey explained. "Bosses and workers can't be friends. They're natural enemies, like, owls and mice."

"Predators," Margalo supplied. "Like me and my sandwich."

"Your sandwich doesn't care if you eat it," Tan said.

"Really? Have you ever asked a sandwich how it feels, sitting there in its paper bag, alone in the dark, in the locker, with the door clanged shut, knowing that the hour of execution is coming closer?"

"Yeah." Tan grinned. "I asked. It didn't answer. So I ate it."

"I have an appointment with Mr. Saunders tomorrow," Mikey said.

"What do you think our chances are?" Tan asked.

Mikey shrugged. "They're worse since this teacher uprising cropped up. He almost wouldn't make any appointment with me. Or, I should say, the secretary tried to refuse to."

Frannie supplied the name. "Mrs. Chambers. She

likes to have everything go her way, but really she's nice."

"She's all right, she's just Hitler reincarnated," Mikey echoed Frannie's earnest voice.

Frannie laughed, but maintained, "They had a hard time figuring out what credits I should get, and Mrs. Chambers was really helpful."

"Yeah, but everybody helps you," Mikey maintained. "So that doesn't count."

"You have the appointment, don't you?" Tan pointed out. "I'll tell people about it. I've always wanted to be a mouthpiece," she said, rising.

Margalo was half-hoping to be able to say to people, later, when they were grown up and Tan was on the cover of *Sports Illustrated*, "She was in my class in school." So now Margalo joked, "I thought you always wanted to be an athlete."

"Yeah, we thought you always wanted to be Vanessa Williams," Mikey added.

Tan corrected her. "That's Venus."

"I know that." Mikey smiled her *Gotcha* smile. "It was a joke. You didn't get it."

"Or Serena," Tan deadpanned and returned to her own table.

Mikey got back to her own interests. "So you need

140

to have all of your arguments all ready to present to Mr. Saunders," she told Margalo.

The next day, they filed into the principal's office, Frannie first, Mikey in the middle, and then Margalo. Mikey carried the petition, all six pages. Mr. Saunders stood up behind his desk, to welcome them. "Frances," he said, sounding a little surprised, as if he wouldn't expect to see Frannie in his office. Or, maybe, in this company? "Michelle," he said, sounding unsurprised.

"Mikey," she reminded him.

"Yes, Mikey. And—?"

"Margalo Epps," Margalo told him, and he nodded, his suspicions confirmed.

Then he sat down behind his big desk. They stood in a line facing him.

"So you're not getting enough competition in your lives," he joked at them, before he switched over to seriousness. "We've only got a few minutes, so let me look at this petition." He shared a friendly, indulgent smile out equally between the three of them, playing no favorites. Mikey did not smile back.

Margalo didn't know what he saw to make him smile like that, except three very different seventh-grade girls, Frannie with her pleasant expression, dressed in a simple khaki skirt and a pale blue blouse; Mikey in her usual cargoes and gray T-shirt; Margalo in a long black skirt with a wide-collared, rose-colored blouse. Frannie looked like somebody left over from the fifties, Mikey like somebody left over from fifth grade, and Margalo—she hoped—like some actress left behind when the theater company left town, some French actress. She tucked her hair behind her ears and watched Mr. Saunders read the petition.

He read the paragraph at the top, slowly. Then he ran his eyes over the columns of signatures, thirty per page, in two neat columns of fifteen each. He read each signature on each of the six pages.

Margalo had time to look around and notice that the office of the principal of a junior high was larger than the office of an elementary school principal. Mr. Saunders had room for a big desk and a set of four upholstered chairs set around a square table. He had a rug on his floor and photographs on his walls. Trophies and books divided the bookcase space about equally between them.

There was a thermos jug and a tray of mugs set out on a side table, with a bowl of sugar packets, a jar of creamer, and wooden stirrers in a Styrofoam cup. Margalo wondered if he was about to have a party, and they were interrupting. Then Mr. Saunders cleared his throat, and gathered the sheets of paper together into a pile.

The first thing he said was, "I don't see any eighth-grade names here." Before they could respond to that criticism, he went on. "Thank you for bringing this to me. Is there anything else?"

Margalo almost applauded. Machiavelli would have been impressed. Mr. Saunders was really good at being principal. But Machiavelli would have been impressed by Margalo, too, when she just stood there, visibly expecting the principal to say more.

"Well?" he finally said, looking at them over his handful of petitions, visibly expecting that they would have left by now.

She almost hated to disappoint him, but she answered, "We were pretty sure you'd want to hear our reasons."

"Oh. Well, yes." He looked at his watch. "Of course."

"Because we know you want to be fair," Margalo told him.

"Well, yes. Of course I do."

"And hear both sides," Margalo added, "before you make up your mind."

She could almost see Mr. Saunders un-making-up his mind, taking it apart like a Tinker toy windmill, as he sat back to hear them out.

They had agreed that after Margalo's introduction, Mikey should go first. So Mikey did. "It's not fair," she said, "when people who are as good as other people don't get to play on a team just because they aren't eighth graders. Also," Mikey said, "the teams aren't as good as they would be if you picked from all the best players, not just the eighth grade's best. So it would be good for school spirit, too," she concluded.

Mr. Saunders waited several seconds before responding. "I hear what you're saying, Mikey. You're a good athlete, aren't you?"

"That's not the point," Mikey argued.

"Isn't it?" he asked, and since it was Mikey, she had to answer, "It's not the *only* point."

"But I didn't know you played basketball," Mr. Saunders said. "Will we also see you playing baseball in the spring?"

"Tennis," Mikey said, brief and furious. "I play in the county league."

"Really?" he said. "Then you're familiar with age restrictions in sports."

"That doesn't make it fair to keep seventh graders off school teams," Mikey maintained.

"It does, however, make it common practice," the principal argued.

Margalo's role was the good cop. (They hadn't planned any role for Frannie; they just took her along because when Frannie was along, things went better.) So Margalo didn't hesitate to take over from Mikey. "Sometimes, it's a good time to change common practice. Like"—she had looked this up, after her stepfather suggested the comparison last night at supper—"when they decided Jackie Robinson could play for the Red Sox. There had never been an African-American in the major leagues before."

"I know baseball history," Mr. Saunders said. "But you aren't trying to claim—"

"No, sir," Margalo answered, throwing in a "sir" so he wouldn't notice that she'd interrupted. "I was just thinking about the effect on the team, and the whole game of baseball, when that change happened. I don't know who the person was who made that decision?"

Mr. Saunders didn't know, either. "Owners and

manager together, is my guess. That's an interesting question."

"If you let seventh graders play on the basketball teams, everybody would feel that good about you."

"Not the eighth graders," Mr. Saunders pointed out.

"Not *this* year's eighth graders, maybe," Margalo pointed out.

"Another interesting point you've made . . . Margalo, is it?" Mr. Saunders said. "I'll certainly think about this, girls. Although in all fairness, I'll also ask the eighth grade what their feeling about the situation is."

"Of course," Frannie agreed. "It would be selfish of us not to find out what they want."

"I *know* what they want," Mikey protested.

"And I know what *you* want," Mr. Saunders told her. He stood up again, hinting again that they should leave. Also, they could hear loud voices beyond the closed office door. "I assure you, I'll give thought to your proposal, and consult some people, and let you know ASAP what I decide. I should warn you, however"—he smiled—"not to get your hopes up."

"I know," Frannie agreed, with her own sympathetic smile. "It's hard getting people to change, isn't it?"

They filed out, almost swept back into the office by a group of four teachers, one of them Mr. Cohen, who burst into the room to let Mr. Saunders know that, "Enough is enough," and that, "We've talked to parents," as if the three seventh-grade girls were not even there, and that, "You're looking down the barrel of a strike, sir."

It was during an all-school assembly, held first period the next Wednesday, which was the Wednesday of Thanksgiving vacation, that Mr. Saunders announced his decision. It was almost a week since they had taken the petition to him.

He held the pages up as he reached the conclusion of his brief remarks. "So have a good holiday, boys and girls, relax, recharge your batteries, and I'll see you again next Monday. But before you break for your committee assignments and drama rehearsals," he told the assembled seventh and eighth graders, "I'm sorry to tell you that I have had to decide against allowing seventh graders to play on the West basketball teams."

He didn't sound sorry, but nobody raised a hand to tell him that. A few eighth-grade boys clapped.

Mr. Saunders said, "I thought long and hard about

this proposal, which has some real merit, but I am not convinced it would be good for West Junior High to make that change." He looked over his audience. "On a happier topic, I want to tell you that I'm pleased to hear how well things are moving forward, on both the dramatic and the dance fronts. And I for one am looking forward to the first bake sale. When will that be? Mrs. Draper?"

The home ec teacher stood up among her homeroom to announce that the bake sales were scheduled to start on the first Friday in December. "So bring good appetites and your spare change," she urged everybody. She looked around at all of the unresponsive faces, and all the bored ones, and all of the half-asleep ones, as well as Mikey's unsurprised, cross one and Margalo's self-congratulatory one, and came to rest on Frannie's smiling one. Mrs. Draper couldn't help but smile back at Frannie. "We're looking forward to our bake sale," Mrs. Draper announced.

The seventh graders were very disappointed. Apparently, as Mikey and Margalo discovered, people had expected Mr. Saunders to grant them their petition. "Too bad, Mikey," Ronnie commiserated, and so did Derry, except that like everything Derry said, it sounded like a question. "I thought he'd sign it, I really did?" Two of the jockettes came up to offer sympathy, "You tried."

"S'okay," Mikey mumbled in response. Of course they had never expected to be given permission to play basketball, but she had to pretend. If Margalo was right—and Margalo had been right so far!—Mikey could hope that this basketball *no* would lead to a tennis *yes*. So Mikey was having a little trouble remembering to look disappointed.

"After all your hard work," many girls said to Margalo. Some of them she knew, and some she didn't, except for their names.

"Bad timing," she said, accepting disappointment with visible maturity. Invisibly, she was not one whit disappointed. She had been one hundred percent right about the outcome. Mr. Saunders had turned them down, and many more seventh graders knew who she was. Things had worked out just the way she'd thought they would.

At lunch in the cafeteria—Spanish rice and sausage patties, the one suspiciously orange and the other dismally brown—more people came up to offer sympathy. Even some of the preppies came by, although not Heather McGinty, to address words to one another over Mikey's and Margalo's heads, but still in their general direction. "It's not fair. Not fair at all."

Mikey and Margalo mumbled and nodded, not unhappy to have everybody on their side, for about the first time in living memory.

"We can try again next year," Frannie said to them just as Louis Caselli, who just happened to be there at the same time as Frannie, said, "You blew it, Meeshelle." Then he turned to Frannie to ask, "Why did we try to get seventh graders on the team when next year we'll be the eighth graders and that would mean some of us would have been cut?"

She explained it patiently. "Because it's the right thing to do. Don't you want to make things righter in the world, Louis?" she asked him.

He didn't want to say yes, because it was wimpy and do-goody and uncool; but he wanted to say yes to Frannie Arenberg so that she would like him and admire him. So all he could say was, "As if."

"We just have to keep on trying," Frannie smiled at him.

Louis looked around, in hope that nobody was watching, but he couldn't help smiling back.

"Because don't you think the worst thing is giving up?" Frannie asked.

Louis nodded his head. He didn't dare look into her face for very long.

Margalo was enjoying this. "Would you have made a seventh and eighth grade team, Louis?" She was pretty sure he wouldn't have.

He had no trouble looking right at Margalo, glaring hard. "Just because I'm not a wimp, like you."

"You know that I don't play team sports," Margalo answered, and looked at Frannie to add, "Louis and us were in the same school for fifth and sixth grades."

"So you're old friends," Frannie said. Then she looked at Louis's face, and at Mikey's face, and at Margalo's face, and added, "Or not."

"Not," Mikey agreed.

"I'll second that," Louis said, with so much feeling that Frannie laughed, and that, too, made him flush. "Porky and me—we're like matter and anti-matter," he added, and then left.

Margalo asked Frannie if she was going to sit down, but Frannie wasn't. She had promised to eat lunch with some Heathers and the Aceys. "So I'll see you two in seminar?" Seminar was their last class before early dismissal for the holiday.

"Or next week," Mikey said. "In case of disaster. I live in hope of disaster."

Frannie laughed again. "You don't mean that." She walked away, carrying her tray out in front of her.

"Oh, yeah?" Mikey called after Frannie. "I live in hope of disaster and I'm almost always disappointed."

Tan plunked herself down at the table. "You know why he waited until today, don't you? Don't you? Because," she answered her own question, "by the time school starts again next week, nobody will care anymore. It'll be forgotten. Like last year's record breaker. But if the teachers can get what they want, why can't we?" she demanded. "Anyway, you tried, Mikey. I'm glad we tried, at least." She got up as suddenly as she had sat down, and strode off.

"She'd have made the basketball team," Mikey said. "No question."

"Would you have?"

"Probably. What I lack in skill I make up for in aggression." Mikey smiled. "Listen, Margalo, my grandmother's staying until Saturday afternoon; do you want to sleep over Saturday night? If you come in time for lunch, you can meet her."

"I'll ask. I don't know if Steven and Aurora need me to baby-sit. Maybe you can come to my house."

Mikey was shaking her head. "No, you *have* to

come to mine. We have to practice chocolate chip cookies. For the bake sale, remember?"

Then they were interrupted by Hadrian Klenk, who stood in front of their table, facing them red-faced. Hadrian's hair had spiky cowlicks, and he had jammed his hands into his pockets. "About your petition," he said. "I'm sorry, Mikey. And you, too, Margalo, because Frannie said you wrote it."

"You didn't even sign it," Mikey told Hadrian.

"Nobody asked me."

"Nobody asked anybody," Mikey said.

"I did," Margalo told her.

"Sometimes," Hadrian reminded Mikey, "people don't want other people even to sign their petitions. And other people had better be careful, because sometimes, people can be mean. If they try to sign the petitions. But you should have used stronger graphics," he said, as if this was the really important part of what he had come to say. "I don't know what software program you have, Mikey, but the pages could have had a much more effective layout. Did you think about splitting the text? Or using a border, or a background design, to catch attention? Or a font that looks more official, more like a real petition, like the Declaration of Independence, maybe older, like the Magna Carta, maybe—"

"Slow down," Margalo advised him.

Hadrian stopped talking.

And stood there, silent.

Until after a while, he said, "I could show you. And you, too, Margalo."

"Sure," Mikey said, and then he did leave, and Mikey said, "unless you think we'd do better with brownies. Or maybe peanut butter cookies? Which do you think are my best cookies, start with that. Which, Margalo?"

Margalo offered Mikey a couple of Oreos, which is what she had in her lunch that day. Then she offered her orange sections. They were discussing the various cookies Mikey made, or could learn to make, when Hadrian Klenk rushed back to their table. It couldn't have been much more than ten minutes he had been gone.

"Look." He put three sheets of paper down in front of them. "It's not exactly right, because—my program at home is better, but you can see how different—" He was as excited as a kid in a TV ad, dragging his parents into Disney World. "Which one do you prefer?" he asked, pushing the three petition pages toward Mikey.

"I'd have to think," Margalo said, but Mikey didn't hesitate. "That one."

Hadrian picked it up. Studied it. "Okay," he said, and rushed off.

"He'll be back," Margalo warned Mikey.

"We'll be gone," Mikey said. "But his did look more official."

"Is he a computer genius?"

"How would I know?"

"The poor little guy's got a crush on you," Margalo observed.

"Too bad for him," Mikey said.

11

California,
Here I (don't) Come

"She liked you. She's pretty funny, isn't she," Mikey greeted Margalo. It wasn't a question.

And that was lucky, because in one afternoon—before Margalo had to be home to baby-sit her younger half sister and half brother—she couldn't begin to figure out Mikey's famous grandmother. Who dyed her hair.

"She liked me?"

Mikey explained Margalo's charms. "You're my best friend."

"I'm your only friend."

"That's why we think when I go stay with her next summer, you should come, too."

Margalo stopped. Dead. In her tracks.

After going on for a few steps, Mikey turned around. "What's the matter?"

Tanisha Harris went by, turned to say, "Neat pants," to Margalo.

"You liked her okay, didn't you?" Mikey demanded.

Margalo nodded. She knew she could never go to California. Steven and Aurora couldn't afford a plane ticket to California. But being invited to go was almost as good, and just as dazzling. She'd never even gotten as close as a chance, before.

Casey Wolsowski came up to ask, "Are those capri pants? Where'd you find them?" but Margalo wasn't about to say. "Wouldn't you like to know?" she asked, Miss Mysteriosa. When Casey had mock-punched Margalo's arm and then walked away, Margalo went back to being dazzled.

California. The Pacific Ocean. Maybe an earthquake. Movie stars. "I can't," she said, "but—"

Mikey interrupted. "Why not?"

Sometimes, Mikey was just stupid.

"Don't you want to?"

"I can't afford it. Crud, Mikey. Let's go in," Margalo said, and they pulled open the big school doors, to enter the long school week.

"Those pants look dumb," Mikey remarked at the same time someone walking by, one of the Barbies, said to her friends, "D'you think I'd look good in capris? Or are my thighs too fat?"

"Your thighs are too fat!" Mikey yelled, and got herself a dirty look. "Well, they are," Mikey maintained to Margalo. "And I still don't like them," she said, staring at Margalo's black capri pants. "I don't care if everybody else in the world does, I don't."

Why am I not surprised? Margalo chose not to ask out loud. Mikey had no taste. As in, No Taste.

"You don't think I have any taste," Mikey accused her as they put lunch and books into their lockers.

"Not true." Margalo grinned. "I think you have bad taste."

"Then explain why I'm such a good cook," Mikey countered. "Did Aurora say you can come home to bake with me on Thursday?"

"I'll ask her tonight, when Steven will be there. He'll think it's okay. I didn't have time yesterday," Margalo reminded Mikey. She'd spent Sunday at Mikey's house, practicing making cookies. Mr. Elsinger had practiced eating them. They'd both done okay at their jobs. In fact, Margalo was looking forward to impressing her family when she made chocolate chip cookies, from scratch.

"Tell her we'll only be alone for a couple of hours," Mikey said. "Dad will come home early."

"I don't blame her for worrying," Margalo defended her mother.

"I don't, either. But I *will*, if her worrying keeps us from making cookies. My cookies are going to be really good," Mikey announced. "And everyone knows that most of the rest of the stuff is going to be made by mothers, anyway, so that's even better. It'll be okay with Aurora," Mikey decided. Then she went back to her main concern of the morning. "If you weren't always buying new clothes, you'd have the money to come to California with me."

Margalo just stared. Mikey didn't get it. She didn't know that sometimes people could work and work and barely earn enough to get by—to feed, clothe, and house themselves and their children. She didn't know how much cheaper margarine was than butter. She didn't know that you could get a whole grocery bag of clothes for only a dollar, if you knew where to shop. There was so much Mikey didn't know, she didn't even know how much she didn't know.

At the look on Margalo's face, Mikey shifted the subject back to baking. "Dad's taking me shopping Wednesday. We *could* cook at your house, but I'm not sure about Aurora's oven. The oven could make a difference, how much I'm not sure. It's not all that easy to—"

Margalo was destined never to hear what it was that Mikey didn't think was all that easy because just then Hadrian Klenk—still in his Polartec jacket—rushed up to them, breathing heavily. "I'm glad I caught you, Mikey. And you, too, Margalo. Look at this—" he said, dropping his knapsack down at his feet right there in the middle of the hall, and rooting around in it to pull out a long, legal-sized manila file folder, labeled MIKEY'S PETITION.

People milled around them, getting to homeroom, to their lockers, to where their friends had already gotten to. Hadrian didn't notice.

"What's with you, creep?" a couple of boys asked, almost tripping over him.

Hadrian was opening up the folder.

A couple of girls maneuvered around him. "Hadrian!" they objected in high voices, and *"Honestly!"* they said to one another.

He *was* in the way, but it wasn't as if he was blocking the whole hall. It wasn't as if you couldn't get around him as he held up a sheet of heavy parchment paper. "Look, Mikey. And you, too, Margalo."

The word "Petition" at the top of the paper looked as if it had been written with a quill pen, the ink was so black, the letters so dark and thick. Little curlicues decorated the start and end of the word. It looked like something written by Thomas Jefferson, or any other one of the Founding Fathers.

Underneath, in smaller size but in the same old-fashioned script, Hadrian had rewritten Margalo's paragraph. Now it started out, "Know by all men present that we, the students of the seventh grade at West Junior High School . . ." It went on in the same style, as if it were over two hundred years old.

"It's just a model," Hadrian explained. "To show what else you could have done. I know it's too late," he apologized.

Margalo was impressed. "Did you write this out by hand?"

"How could I do that? My graphics program has lots of fonts, and once I had the right paper . . . see, Mikey," he explained, "It's not just the font that gets you the formal effect. It has a lot to do with the kind of paper you use. That, and the size of the type, the darkness of the ink. And the spacing, too, the margins at the sides and top and bottom, between the words, between the letters. All of that can be adjusted." He pointed to each feature as he mentioned it. "I think it's the H that really makes this font look good. And the lowercase e," he said, his finger picking out those letters. "Don't you think, Mikey? And you, too, Margalo."

The bell rang, and Hadrian bent down to collect his scattered possessions, but he looked up to say, "I'm sorry it's too late."

"Probably it wouldn't have made any difference," Margalo consoled him as they moved quickly away. It wasn't smart to be seen standing around talking with Hadrian Klenk.

"Maybe it would have," he called after them.

At lunch, Hadrian came up to them in the cafeteria line, to show them the same design, with the letters of the heading shadowed by bright red. "This was another idea I had," he said, trailing behind them. "I kind of thought it might be better, don't you, Mikey? And you, too, Margalo."

At the end of school, he was waiting when they emerged from homeroom, to show them, "The best one of all, tell me what you think, Mikey. And you—" But they just brushed past Hadrian Klenk, pretending not to notice him.

Mikey put their opinion into words. "Just because he's so much younger, and probably a genius, doesn't mean he gets to pester me."

"Do you think he really could be a genius?" Margalo asked, looking back at him thoughtfully. It was normal for geniuses to be out of it—out of touch with reality, out-to-lunch, way out—in school. But in the long run—and school was the short run, she knew that—the geniuses were better to be friends with than the normal, popular people. She thought about returning to hear what Hadrian wanted to say, but Mikey's attention had moved on, or, more accurately, it had headed back, toward California. "What about baby-sitting? For money," she explained. "For your plane ticket."

"Aurora can't afford to pay—"

"No, I mean for other people. You can charge a lot, especially if you've taken the baby-sitting course at the library."

"But I haven't."

"But you could. It's free."

"Anyway, how would I get people to hire me?"

"Put up notices, in the library, maybe at the super-market? Or"—and Mikey's face lit up with interest—"this is a really good idea. At your doctor's. And I'll do it at mine. I'll talk to Aurora about you doing baby-sitting work. She thinks I'm a live wire and she'd want you to be able to come out to Grammy's with me. Let me do the talking, Margalo, okay?"

Margalo just nodded, because—for the first time—she was thinking about how Mikey wasn't even slowed down by the difficulties of being a kid. She just crashed on through them, to get what she wanted.

Mikey was the only person Margalo ever wished she was more like.

"You know what I think?" Margalo asked Mikey, at lunch the next day.

"Ask me if I care," Mikey answered.

"You should," Margalo answered. That was all she said.

Mikey waited, pretending not to wait. She pulled her braid around to the front, as if she was checking for split ends, as if she cared if her ends split. She tossed her braid back over her shoulder and turned her attention to the noodle casserole on her plate. This was served mounded up into a hill shape. Chunks of pale yellowy orange carrots were piled beside it, with a piece of buttered bread resting over them. There were specks of beige somethings in the casserole, and Mikey picked one out with her fork and held it out before Margalo like some scientist with an unknown species of bug, asking his fellow scientist for an identification. "All right, all right," Mikey said. "Why should I care? What *should* I care about? What now?"

Margalo knew a victory when she won it. "If Hadrian really *is* a genius, maybe we should be nice to him," she said.

"No way," Mikey explained. "All he thinks about is—he's obsessive."

"Although he's seriously weird," Margalo pointed out, arguing with herself about this.

"I don't mind weird," Mikey said. "People think I'm weird," she reminded Margalo, adding, "They're wrong, but they don't know it. *You're* the one of us who's weird," she concluded.

"Says who?"

"You just pretend you aren't."

Well, Margalo couldn't argue about that. A lot of her whole life was a costume she put together, and put on. She was pretty good at it, too, getting people to think they were seeing what she wanted them to see when they looked at her. "So what?" she asked.

"So what I want to hear about now is what Aurora said after I went home and you had one of your dinner table talks about California," Mikey said.

But before Margalo could tell her the bad news, there was Hadrian Klenk, back again, another sheet of paper in his hand to show them. The lettering on it was of the old-fashioned kind that looks like it would be used for writing fairy tales, tall and stiff, with little thin echoes for the crossbars. "What do you think of this?" he asked Mikey, bending over a little to lay the paper out beside Mikey's tray.

"Give it a rest, Hadrian," Mikey said but, "No, what do you think? I changed it, see?" he insisted.

Hadrian had reversed the design. He had put the places for signatures at the top, with the statement of what the petition was for beneath them. Beneath all of that, at the bottom center of the page, he had printed out in letters large enough to be a newspaper headline, PETITION.

"Okay, so you changed it," Mikey acknowledged, and went back to her lunch.

"No, it's really interesting," Margalo said, pulling the paper over to look at it. "This way, the signatures are more important, because they come first."

"That's what I thought," Hadrian said.

"You're good at this," Margalo said.

Hadrian looked hopefully back to Mikey.

"Okay, so I like it," she said. "So what?"

"You do?" he answered.

"But we're *done* with this petition, Hadrian."

"I know that." He picked up his piece of paper, folded it, and jammed it into his rear pocket. "But there'll be more, you know. Before we get out of school, there's every likelihood of more petitions. Although I don't know yet what they'll be for," he said, speaking to himself, really, as he wandered away.

Margalo picked up the second half of her sandwich, leftover turkey and mayonnaise.

"I don't have a turkey sandwich," Mikey pointed out.

Margalo chewed. "Too bad." She didn't think Mikey would care but she told her anyway, "I went shopping with Aurora and Esther on Saturday, at the New-to-You."

Mikey wouldn't even fake interest. So Margalo didn't tell her about the incredible sweater she'd found, with an Italian name on its label, costing only one dollar and twenty-five cents, which was more expensive than most of the other selections at that store. Mikey would find out about the sweater soon enough.

Frannie came by, sat down beside Mikey, said hey, and declined Margalo's offer of a Fig Newton. Mikey took two. "What time are you assigned to the bake sale table?" Frannie asked.

The way the committee had divided up the assignments, the people who baked for that day didn't have to sell, and the people who were assigned to the table didn't bake.

"We're baking," Mikey said. "We're always going to be baking."

"Can you do that?" Frannie wondered. "Nobody else is."

Mikey just smiled, a *Just-watch-me* smile, and Frannie laughed. "Did Hadrian show you his new design for the petition?" she asked now. "He's really good with graphics."

On Friday morning, both Mikey and Margalo carried a big shopping bag into the school. Each shopping bag had three shoe boxes piled up in it. Each shoe box held two dozen chocolate chip cookies. "Which means that together we're a gross," Mikey said to Margalo.

"Better than being plain gross," Margalo answered as they went down the hall to the principal's office. To create a larger desire for her cookies by making it look like there weren't very many, Mikey had decided to leave one of the shopping bags in the office, with the secretary. She hadn't told Mrs. Chambers about this yet.

Knapsacks in one hand and shopping bags in the other, they stood in front of the secretary's desk. Mrs. Chambers was on the phone and tried to learn without talking to them what they wanted, so she could refuse without interrupting her call. She put a hand up to her forehead as if she was feeling for a temperature. Mikey and Margalo shook their heads. No, they weren't feverish. Mrs. Chambers pointed down her throat with two fingers, and they shook their heads. No, they weren't nauseated; or maybe no, they didn't have sore throats. Mrs. Chambers, waiting with the phone held up against one ear, seemed puzzled. She wrote *Cramps?* on her little notepad, turned it around to face them; and they shook their heads, no cramps. With all of that information gathered, all of it negative, Mrs. Chambers made her decision. With her free hand she waved them away, *Go away, go to home-room, the bell's about to ring.*

Mikey and Margalo shook their heads, No.

Finally, Mrs. Chambers said into the phone, "We'll give the class a study hall in the library until you get here. As soon as you can," she said, and hung up the phone. "Then *what?*" she asked Margalo.

"Will you keep this shopping bag in your office, please? It's for the bake sale table."

"Mrs. Draper is in charge of bake sale goods," Mrs. Chambers said.

"They'll be safer with you," Margalo said.

Mrs. Chambers agreed about that, but said, "I can't let you. What if everybody wanted to?"

"But everybody doesn't," Mikey said.

"I don't need added responsibilities," Mrs. Chambers said.

"They're marked with our initials," Mikey pointed out.

The telephone rang, Mr. Saunders called out, "Marie?" from behind the open door into his office, then Mr. Cohen entered to find out where his home-room students who were scheduled for Mrs. Sanabria's gym class should go for first period, since she was out sick, and another teacher entered with two eighth-grade boys who glared at one another across the width of the teacher.

Mrs. Chambers punched a button and picked up the ringing phone. "West Junior High School, good morning."

"Thanks a lot," Margalo said, and set her shopping bag down behind the secretary's desk. The bag was labeled ME. Each shoebox in it was labeled ME.

Out in the corridor, Mikey told Margalo, "You take my shopping bag to Mrs. Draper's room."

"Why don't you?"

"I'll get your books and put your lunch in your locker." Mikey reached out for Margalo's knapsack, passing over her own shopping bag.

"I want to get my own books," Margalo protested. "I know what I need. Why don't you run your own errands?"

"Jumping Jehoshaphat, Margalo, you're supposed to be so smart about people. You know what'll happen to cookies people think I made. Just do it my way, okay? It's only for this week, until the cookies sell themselves."

Well, there was a seventh-grade form of the grade

school cootie game, Margalo couldn't deny it. But, "Why does your way mean I have to run around doing your errands? And probably getting in trouble because probably I'll be late to homeroom," she groused.

"You will if you don't get going," Mikey agreed.

Mikey had a whole marketing strategy worked out. Her idea was to give Mrs. Draper half of the cookies—three shoe boxes—for the lunchtime bake sale table. Then, at the end of lunch, when those three boxes had sold out, Margalo would bring one more to the table. They would bring the last two boxes out for the after-school sale.

Mikey had explained it all to Margalo, at length. "My cookies will be better than anything else they have, so everybody will want them. When they run out, people will want them more. Because," she explained, "consumers want what they think is hard to get. Like Beanie Babies, like Pokémon dolls."

"I never wanted any of those."

"I didn't say you, I said people."

"I'm people," Margalo pointed out, on principle.

"Leaping Lizards, Margalo," Mikey argued, exasperated. "What is with you? You know I'm right."

"I'm just helping you stay calm," Margalo said.

"How can you help me stay calm by picking stupid fights with me?" Mikey demanded.

"By burning up your excess energy," Margalo explained.

"This is just basic marketing, creating a need," Mikey explained.

Mikey talked confident, but she refused to go anywhere near the bake sale table. They had stapled blue and white crepe paper streamers to hang down over the flowered sheet that Casey Wolsowski's mother had donated to the decorating committee, and Mikey said she didn't want to be anywhere near it. "What if cute is contagious?" she asked, and Margalo promised, "You're immune." Her cookies were being grabbed up as soon as the boxes were opened, but all Mikey would say about it was, "They're jerks to sell my cookies for only ten cents. I'd charge at least fifty cents. For the bake sale. I bet I could get a dollar on the street."

She and Margalo were pretending not to care, although both of them felt entirely victorious, especially because some time before the end of first lunch, word got out that those were Mikey Elsinger's chocolate chip cookies that were the most popular item on the table.

"I could make the committee buy my cookies," Mikey realized.

"Are you trying to increase your unpopularity?" Margalo demanded.

"As if I care."

"Yeah, but the petition changed—"

"The petition wasn't about getting popular. It was about tennis, only nobody knows that. Except you."

"And besides," Margalo returned to the point, "the cookies donated to the bake sale are to benefit the class. You *can't* charge for them."

"I worked it out," Mikey told her. "It costs thirteen cents a cookie—say, fifteen cents, to be on the safe side—and at fifty cents apiece, that's thirty-five cents' profit for each cookie. So selling a gross would get me about fifty dollars in profit. Actually, fifty dollars and forty cents, as I worked it out. If I charged the committee even just a quarter a cookie, I'd make money."

"If you tried it, you'd make nothing but trouble."

"If I made money, I could buy you a ticket to California. I looked it up on the Net; it's four hundred seven dollars. Round trip. Booked more than three weeks in advance. Nonreturnable."

That stopped Margalo, shut her up, because if

there was any way she could pay for a plane ticket out to California, and stay with Mrs. Elsinger for free . . . but that was more hope than she could tolerate, and besides, Mr. Saunders would never let Mikey do that, and besides, the dance was only a couple of months away, minus Christmas vacation, so they didn't have enough bake sales to cover the price of a ticket, anyway.

"There's nowhere near enough time, Mikey. I thought you were so good at math."

"You know," Mikey snapped at her, "computers aren't the only kind of geniuses people can be."

Margalo bit back, "Now you're a genius? I guess that explains why nobody likes you."

"You like me," Mikey reminded her. She proved her point. "You'd come to California with me if you could, wouldn't you?"

12
Margalo Solo

Margalo knew ahead of time that Mikey was going to be absent on Monday. Mikey came down with the flu at her mother's, who returned Mikey on Saturday so she could be sick at home. On Sunday night Mikey called Margalo to tell her this. "How bad do you feel?" Margalo asked.

"You have to get my assignments," Mikey said.

"I wanted you to bring me one of your T-shirts," Margalo complained. "For this new sweater—"

"All of the classes. Not just the ones we're in together."

"You *will* lend me one, won't you?"

"Don't think you can keep me off high honor roll by pretending to forget," Mikey said.

"One of the gray ones," Margalo said.

"I've got three of the five classic flu symptoms. No nausea. No muscle aches."

"Maybe Frannie will eat lunch with me."

Neither one of them asked *Are you listening to me?* They each knew that the other was listening.

"Dad'll come by for my books after work. He's staying home with me tomorrow if my temperature isn't below a hundred."

"Do you think you'll be well enough to come to school on Tuesday?"

"Don't forget."

Margalo felt a little uneasy arriving at West Junior High School when Mikey wasn't going to be there. She scurried down off the bus and scurried right on into the building, went to her locker and then to the library. She could always read something while sitting in the stacks, which was maybe two degrees less obviously unpopular than doing your homework in the library. And she *did* have her civics current events topic to get, too. This was Mr. Cohen's way of getting students to at least look at a daily newspaper.

Margalo usually got her items from the library's copy of the *Monitor* while Mikey—who took her topics from her father's copy of the Sunday *New York*

Times—usually hovered around, interrupting. The *Monitor* had all the big stories on its back page, both national and international, as well as a column of odd facts, like which cities were the most expensive to live in, or if some bank robber had crashed his getaway car right into a police station. Looking for a topic would give Margalo something to do.

But arty-smarty Cassie was sitting at a table with the *Monitor* open in front of her. Margalo got into position, hoping that Cassie wasn't the kind of person who minded people reading over her shoulder.

"Hey, Margalo, what's new?" Cassie asked. She indicated the empty chair beside her. "Park your buns. I guess you have Cohen for civics, too."

Margalo nodded, sat. "Seventh period."

"Weren't you surprised to find him at the head of that army of revolutionaries?" Cassie asked.

"I think *he* was the surprised one," Margalo commented. Cassie thought that was funny, which made it *So far, so good* for Margalo, on her own in junior high for the first time. She looked down at the newspaper. "He lets you bring in arts items?"

Cassie shrugged. "Art's important. *Uncle Tom's Cabin* started a war."

No, it contributed to starting the war, Margalo corrected, but not out loud. Out loud, "I guess you're right," she said. "Or Picasso," she added. You could always mention Picasso and be right about art.

"Exactly," Cassie said, so probably she didn't know anything about Picasso, either. She went back to reading but pointed with a finger to a paragraph, to mark her place, and looked up again to say, "Except he doesn't allow anything about TV. I tried."

Cassie had painted her fingernails a light metallic blue, and they were cut short, not even reaching the tops of her fingers; this was not a look Margalo admired. "Cool nails," she said.

"Okay, I'm done," Cassie announced. "I never spend more than twelve minutes a day on homework. What they get is what they get." She grinned. "Don't you just hate it?"

"School?" Margalo asked, not exactly agreeing with Cassie, not exactly disagreeing.

"Can't you barely wait until we get out?" Cassie commiserated.

"I take it you don't mean just Christmas vacation," Margalo said.

Cassie thought that was funny, too. "Are you taking in that item about gangs in schools?" she asked Margalo now.

179

"Do you think we have gangs here at West?"

"Not so's you'd notice," was Cassie's opinion. "Saunders would be all over them. 'Here at West Junior High we have no gangs, only cliques,'" she said in a soft, saleslady voice.

"Which are just wanna-be gangs," Margalo commented.

"On the nose, Mar," Cassie commented, as if she wasn't, herself, a member of a clique. "I'm taking the article to see what Cohen says."

Frannie approached them and greeted them, asking Margalo if she was finished with the *Monitor*. "Where's Mikey?" she wondered, and Margalo said, "Home sick."

"Tell her I hope she feels better," Frannie said, and wandered back to the table she came from, carrying the paper.

"That girl is so nice," Cassie remarked. "I mean, like, she really is. And pretty, too, isn't she? I shouldn't like her."

"I can't not, either," Margalo agreed. "But, Cassie, how do you get homework essays written in only twelve minutes?"

Cassie liked being asked that question. "I manage. Sometimes, I keep them really short. Short and bril-

180

liant. Or I use an old one. It's not cheating," she assured Margalo, in case Margalo wondered. "It's just—school's a place I'm serving time, like a criminal in the penitentiary, and my crime is being a kid, until I turn sixteen and can go to art school."

"Can you go to art school at sixteen?" Margalo asked, but the bell rang then, so Cassie said, "Talk to you later," and they hurried off to their homerooms.

Definitely *So far, so good.*

Going down the hall toward English class, she greeted Ronnie, "Hihowareyou?" and was answered, "Cool, how're you?" to which her answer was, "I'm cool." Heather McGinty approached them, her face all saddened by fake sympathy, to say, "I meant to tell you how sorry I am that your petition didn't make any difference."

"Yeah, I guess," Margalo said, faking acceptance of the fake sympathy, and added, "I'm sorry your lemon bars didn't sell any better."

Heather accepted that as if she thought she had cornered the insincerity market. "It's funny because my mother's bridge club just loves them, which is why she made them for us. But Frannie bought four, one for each person in her family. She wanted them for Friday dessert. You can tell when someone's mature,"

Heather McGinty informed Ronnie, "by their mature taste."

"Did you guys see the hunk on the cover of the new J.Crew catalog?" Annie Piers asked as she came up to join them.

"No," Margalo said truthfully.

"He's the cutest," Annie said. "I'll bring it in."

"I always think the best-looking guys are the ones in the Brooks Brothers catalog," Lacey said. "Even the old guys in there are handsome, and—they all look so rich."

Margalo's house didn't get any catalogs. Years ago, Aurora had written some special address to cancel all mail-order catalogs, regardless of price, content, or source. Aurora shopped sales, not catalogs. But Margalo agreed with Lacey, anyway, and when Ronnie disagreed, Margalo got pretty emotional. "Holy moley, Ronnie, there's just no comparison."

Ronnie started to giggle. Margalo went right on. "Those J.Crew guys all look so soft. You know? Soft, sensitive types." She was making it up as she went along.

"That's why I like them," Ronnie said, grinning. "You're just arguing for the sake of arguing, Margalo."

"Her and Mikey, they disagree with everybody about everything," Heather McGinty announced. "They just want to be different."

"Of course," Margalo agreed. "Otherwise it would be too boring." And since she was ahead, she detached herself from the group, exiting with Ronnie's comment, "You're just *bad.*"

Everything went along excellently. At noon, Margalo entered the cafeteria, her lunch bag in her hand and an eye out for Tanisha, because she knew Tan from way back. And if Tan's jockette friends refused to welcome Margalo? Well, she could eat standing by her locker, get down at least enough to get through the afternoon before some teacher caught her. After lunch was going to be the worst time, and she could spend that in the library.

But she ran into Casey Wolsowski—literally ran into her back since the girl came to a halt, right in front of Margalo.

"Hunhhph," Margalo said. "Oh, Casey, hihowareyou?"

"Cool," Casey answered, not looking up from the paperback book she was reading.

"What's so good?" Margalo asked, expecting—she didn't know, maybe *Forever,* maybe a Harry Potter.

Casey turned the book over to show her—*Watership Down*.

"My stepbrother's reading that in high school," Margalo said.

"Probably he has my dad for English. This is my second time. In fact," she smiled, half-proud, half-ready to be made fun of, "I finished it yesterday afternoon and started it all over again right away."

"I usually let an hour or two go by before restarting a book," Margalo admitted, which was almost true. "I didn't know you were so good in English," she said to Casey.

"I'm not. I just read. You're the one who's good."

"Not really. Grammar, spelling, you know. The easy stuff."

"That's not the easy stuff," Casey said. They were moving together in the cafeteria line, not that Margalo was going to get anything, and not that Casey noticed. "Have you read this?"

"Howie doesn't share."

"I'll loan it to you when I finish. What about *Lord of the Rings*, if you like fantasy? Do you like fantasy?"

"I like everything," Margalo said, and that was true.

"Try *Lord of the Rings*," Casey said. "But start it on

a Friday, or over vacation. Because you won't want to be interrupted." She put a filled plate on her tray.

Margalo didn't tell Casey she'd read Tolkien's trilogy for the first time this summer, and for the second time, too; she figured, if Casey felt like she'd introduced Margalo to something, she'd like Margalo better.

"How about *The Thirteen Clocks*?" Casey asked now, a book Margalo had never heard of. Casey added a bowl of fruit and two perfectly round cookies—sugar cookies? Nut cookies? Oatmeal cookies? "Aren't you eating?"

Margalo held up her brown bag, a show-and-tell.

"That's smart," Casey remarked, and "See you around," she said, walking off to join the other preppies at Heather McGinty's table, turning back to observe, "You never said what books you like," before turning away again.

Margalo thought she might mention *Jane Eyre*. If she understood Casey, that would be just the book to mention. Meanwhile, she drifted over toward where Tan sat. "Hey, whazzup?" she greeted them, and asked, "Can—?" waving her lunch bag gently in the air, not exactly asking so that they wouldn't have to say exactly no. "Whazzup, Margalo?" Tan asked, indicating an empty seat. "Mikey sick?"

"Flu," Margalo said. "She'll miss practice. She doesn't know about tomorrow."

"She'll be back as soon as she can," Tan said, sure of it. She turned to the girl on her other side to explain, "Margalo and her friend Mikey are the ones who started that basketball petition."

"Hey, whazzup?" the girl greeted Margalo now. "I thought that was Frannie."

"Her, too," Margalo said.

"Frannie's a real good sport," the girl said. "She a friend of yours?"

"Frannie's a friend of everybody's," Margalo said.

"Margalo doesn't play sports," Tan said, grinning now at Margalo, remembering grade school.

"But I'm interested in watching," Margalo answered. "I'm an interested audience. Like, I always wonder about plays. Basketball plays, especially. I always wondered, because you only see the plays in games." (Well, she *had* watched one pro game with Mikey, on TV last year; that counted, didn't it?) "I wondered if you practice the moves. Like dancers, rehearse them until you do them without thinking? Otherwise, how do people get so good at doing the right moves when they're in the middle of a point, or a game?"

"A lot of practice," Tan said, "and talent, too. It's gotta be both, don't you think, Ellie?" she asked her friend, who added, "Also, going with the flow," which Tan thought was, "The same as practice and talent, just different words."

They talked on happily, about scrimmages and whose game was really on, and about how Mikey made a lousy guard but was a natural shot, even though she was too short and chunky, really, for basketball. "But she makes up for it in competitiveness. I guess you're not competitive," Tan said to Margalo, sounding surprised, as if she'd never thought of this before.

Margalo shrugged. If that was what Tan thought, what would be the point of denying it?

"Maybe that's how you and Mikey stay friends," Tan said. "You are still friends, aren't you?"

"Absolutely," Margalo said. Although, she had to admit and she didn't mind admitting to herself, it felt kind of good to have Mikey be absent. It was like Margalo was the only person onstage, the star of the show, when Mikey was home sick; and it looked like she could do just fine, onstage alone.

But Tanisha had reminded her of her responsibility, so she went off to get the homework for Mikey's morning classes, which meant having a reason to talk to even more people, and make her own impression on them.

Mikey was absent again on Tuesday, but, "Getting better. I better get better or we won't have cookies for Friday and that'll interfere with my plan," she had said on the phone. "What do cookies have to do with making high honor roll?" Margalo had asked, and when Mikey said, "No, the California plan," Margalo asked, "You aren't really going to try to *sell* your cookies to the committee, are you?"

"Have some imagination," Mikey had said, then, "I'll call you tomorrow. After school."

So Margalo went in on her own Tuesday morning, again. And she felt that morning like she was in charge of things. She had her connection into every group. Except the Barbies, she thought, taking a look at Rhonda Ransom standing in the hallway among her big-haired, small-waisted, high-heeled friends. But there had to be a way to get connected to a Barbie, because they were just seventh graders, after all. Taking a look, thinking, Margalo wondered if she could figure out what the way might be.

It was when she was banging her locker door shut

that she thought to herself: But I don't want to. And asked herself: So why should I? Just to prove I can?

She talked to Cassie about cappuccino and *Rashomon*, an old Japanese film she hadn't seen, but which David, her film-fanatic stepbrother, maintained was the most perfect movie ever made. Margalo just said what David said, and they never doubted her, the arty-smarties.

She talked to Ronnie about the baby-sitting course at the library, because Ronnie had taken it in sixth grade. The most interesting thing about talking to Ronnie, with Annie Piers and Lacey hanging around, and Casey coming up to say, "Hihowareyou?" and, "Meet me at lunch," was the way Heather McGinty looked nervously over from where she stood between another Heather and a Stacey. Heather kind of moved her mouth into a kind of smile, at Margalo— the friendliness you show to someone you don't personally like, but everybody else might.

At lunch, Margalo sat with Casey, at the end of the preppies' table, talking about books. Casey loaned her a copy of *Watership Down*. "My dad has extra copies, so it's okay. I told him you look like someone who'll take care of a book. You will, won't you?"

"It depends on what you mean by 'take care.'

Because especially a paperback, if you read it, it gets worn out," Margalo pointed out.

"He means, like, leaving it outside, or dropping it in the tub."

"It's been years since I dropped a book in the tub," Margalo said. "What about *Jane Eyre?* Have you read that? Because I bet you'd like it."

"Have you?" Casey asked, and Margalo decided the truth would get her closer than a lie to what she wanted. "I haven't read it yet. I've been waiting for the right time."

"And you think seventh grade is the right time?"

"We could try," Margalo said. "I can get to the library on Saturday. Does your father have a copy?"

"I think so. Hardbound, so it must be one he likes. I won't start reading until Saturday night."

"It's not a race," Margalo pointed out.

"I know, it's just more fun if you're both reading it at the same time."

Margalo asked, "Do you want to say how many pages?"

"This could be fun," Casey said. "We could be like a book club. Nobody else *reads*," she complained, meaning—as Margalo knew—nobody else in her own group of friends.

"Yeah, but at least they think you're smarter because you do," Margalo pointed out.

"They tease me about it," Casey confided.

When Margalo went over to Tanisha to ask about the math assignment, she was with her friend Lauren. "Lauren's the best guard in seventh grade," Tan said, introducing her. "No, *you* are," Lauren argued, and they replayed a couple of points from yesterday's practice. Margalo acted interested in that, acted impressed, acted like she cared.

There was a lot of acting that went into getting less unpopular. It got tiresome, doing all that acting. The trouble with Mikey being home sick was that she wasn't there, in school, to admire Margalo's success, and maybe even be a little jealous. Of course, Mikey jealous was no fun, as in No Fun At All. So maybe it was better not to have her around.

Maybe, but the thing about Mikey also was, she was more interesting than other people.

So okay, she hogged the spotlight. Big deal. Who wanted to fight over stage center, anyway? Not Margalo. Jumping Jehoshaphat! The last thing Margalo wanted was the spotlight always on her. That would just—

With Mikey hogging the spotlight, Margalo could

move around in the shadow, doing whatever she wanted, knowing that all eyes were on Mikey.

So it was good news, wasn't it? when Mikey said she was coming back on Wednesday, and she was going to hand in homework papers so perfect, they would just about guarantee her a place on high honor roll, and she'd been practicing free throws, now that she felt better again. "School is bad enough," Mikey said, "but staying home is even worse." She promised to remember to bring in the T-shirt Margalo had asked her for. Margalo wouldn't tell her why, but Mikey already knew the answer. "It's for one of your outfits," she said. "I bet it is. I bet it's that new sweater you were trying to bore me about."

And that irritated Margalo, because she assumed that Mikey never paid any attention about clothes. She almost wished Mikey would stay out of school longer.

Except that Mikey was the only one who could figure Margalo out. Margalo could get other people to like her, but only Mikey knew her.

13

One (bad) Egg, Poached

Margalo rushed Mikey into the school building and into the girls' bathroom the next morning, not even giving her a chance to off-load books into her locker. "Hey," Mikey protested, "what's with you?" resisting, "Jeepers creepers, Margalo! Take it easy, why don't you?"

Margalo wore Aurora's raincoat, a long, yellow slicker. She had it done up all the way to her neck.

"You expecting an indoor shower?" Mikey asked, sarcastic. She spelled it out, "H.A.H.A.," since Margalo entirely missed the joke.

Margalo had no time for Mikey's bad jokes. "Did you bring it?" She took the gray T-shirt and disappeared into one of the stalls.

Mikey waited, watching a couple of eighth-grade girls comb their hair, put on mascara, paint pouty pink mouths on. *Yoicks!* she thought. *Not me, not ever.* The smell of cigarette smoke rose out of one of the stalls, and, bending over, Mikey saw six feet in three pairs of Nikes, all pointing toward the base of the toilet. *Crud!* she thought. Thick perfume smells mixed in with the tobacco-y air, and Mikey stayed bent over—when they told you how to survive a fire, didn't they say the most oxygen was nearest the floor?

While she was bent over like that, she checked out what Margalo was doing.

Knapsack and raincoat were on the floor, and on top of them some seaweedy brownish-grayish-greenish cloth, some old, used dust rag. Margalo was wearing those capri pants again, and a pair of the clunky black oxfords that were her winter shoes. Margalo's hair came into view as she bent down, and Mikey straightened up fast.

Acting like she didn't even know Mikey, Margalo stepped out of her cubicle and crossed briskly to an empty sink, with the long mirror above it. She reached into her knapsack and pulled out a long, golden tube. She was ignoring Mikey so completely that Mikey pushed her face right up to Margalo's, so close that Margalo's face had to share the mirror with Mikey's.

"What are you doing?"

"Putting on mascara."

"What did you do, steal some from Susannah?"

"As it happens, I borrowed this."

"From who?"

"Her name's Cassie. She's in my math class."

Mikey backed down, backed off. She watched Margalo run the tiny brush up along her upper eyelashes, once, twice, then once down, along the lashes at the bottom of each eye. "That looks dumb," she said, and then, "Who showed you how to do that?"

Margalo didn't answer. When she was done, she turned around and asked Mikey, "What do you think?"

"I think you've lost your mind."

"I mean, what do you think of the sweater."

Then Mikey noticed that Margalo was wearing a long sweater, with a wide gray belt at the waist and big gray buttons up the front. The sweater even had a collar.

The sweater was that dust rag. It really was a strange color, a really strange color, maybe the strangest color that Mikey had ever seen, and for sure the strangest color that West Junior High School had ever seen.

Margalo's hair was the same straight brown, tucked behind her ears in the same way, parted off center like always; the way Aurora cut it. Her eyes were the same brown eyes. She was the same height and non-build as always, the same as last Friday. Nothing had changed about Margalo. But that sweater—the color of pea soup, with some ashes stirred into it, and maybe a few crushed dead leaves added for texture—that sweater made Margalo look like a stranger.

Or was it the mascara?

"Holy moley, Margalo," Mikey said.

"Isn't it great?"

"I don't know why you needed my T-shirt." There was only a tiny gray band of T-shirt showing.

Margalo stood up onto her toes and pulled the sweater down over her thighs. She pulled at the belt a little, moving it around a little, making everything perfect. "What do you think?"

Mikey didn't know what she thought. "You look thirty."

"No, I don't. Maybe nineteen."

"And French."

"Italian. The label's Italian. La Scala."

"Like someone from Rome," Mikey said, trying to name a place exotic enough to explain how Margalo looked. "Or Rio de Janeiro? Sardinia?"

"*Zut, alors!*" Margalo murmured, watching herself in the mirror. Her face had no expression, unless that was a bored-to-death expression on her face. She raised her eyebrows, just a little. "I look that good?"

"You don't look like you go to West Junior High," Mikey said. "What do you call that color, dog's throw-up?"

"I knew you wouldn't like it."

"Well, you were right."

"Because it's so great-looking," Margalo said. "Follow me. Watch. Listen. Learn." At the door, she turned around and said to Mikey, "Bring my stuff, will you?" Then she pulled open the door to the bathroom and swept out into the hallway as if she were Queen Elizabeth I about to go sink the entire Spanish Armada single-handed.

Grumbling, like the dwarf who was the queen's jester, Mikey picked up the extra knapsack, and the raincoat, and followed Margalo out the door.

Margalo swept on along, Queen Margalo, who

knew that everybody was watching her, and wishing they were her. And everybody *did* look at her, as if she really was a queen, or at least popular.

Trailing along behind that long, narrow back with the wide belt snug around the waist, Mikey started to enjoy herself. She knew where Margalo shopped, and all of the attention Margalo was getting was pretty funny, when you thought of that. Most of these admiring people were happy to spend a hundred dollars of some parent's money on the exact same sweater every one of them, practically, was wearing, and none of them had people turning to watch them parade down the hall.

So Mikey was pretty proud of Margalo, and pretty pleased to be part of the act. Margalo stopped in front of their lockers. That dog puke color actually did look good on her. How did she do it?

Although, Mikey wasn't about to let Margalo get away with acting stuck up to *her*: "I'm not your dwarf," she said, passing over the knapsack, and the raincoat. "And I don't see why you had to have my T-shirt, anyway."

Margalo unbuttoned the big top button, showing just a little more of the gray underneath, and looked even better. She grinned, in total victory.

Mikey grumbled, dumped her books around, pulled out homework papers.

"Rats on you, Mikey," Margalo said. "If you're going to be like that. Just because I—"

"What, because you *what?*" Mikey demanded.

"Look so good," Margalo said.

"Just wash it before you bring it back," Mikey answered.

In homeroom, too, Margalo had everyone's attention. "You're a real *femme fatale*," Mikey leaned over to whisper to Margalo, who just nodded her head like somone who has absolutely aced a math test. "You and Jessica Rabbit."

Margalo tried not to laugh, and failed. Mikey felt better.

When they met by their lockers at midmorning, Mikey noticed even Heather McGinty sidling up to take a look at Queen Margalo, who had Annie Piers and Casey Wolsowski hovering around her. "*Tell*, Margalo," Annie was begging, and Casey was saying, "*Don't* tell, Margalo. Nobody else would look good in it, anyway."

Mikey clanged her locker door shut and exited the scene. Margalo didn't even notice if she was there or not.

But by lunchtime, everything had changed.

Mikey didn't know how she knew this, but she was sure of it. It was like a tennis match, when the person who was winning—say, Serena Williams—just starts losing points against, maybe, Arantza Sanchez-Vicario. Everybody in the stands can tell that everything has shifted, although nobody knows why, especially Serena. The announcers stop talking about "the Williams serve" and start talking up "the Sanchez-Vicario scramble." Even people sitting at home in front of their television sets can tell that things have shifted.

Things had shifted against Margalo, Mikey could tell.

People still looked at her, but then they looked away quickly, as if they didn't want to be seen staring—the way people don't want to be caught staring at a homeless person. But how could Margalo go from queen to homeless person in half a morning? And why didn't Margalo say anything?

They moved along the line, Mikey behind Margalo—even though Margalo was only there while Mikey got her lunch. Grilled cheese sandwiches and french fries today, a crisp brown fatty meal; maybe Mikey *would* try some salad. She could top it with peas; peas had flavor.

Maybe she'd go on a diet and never eat lunch again, and get as thin as Margalo so she could look like some thirty-year-old French model. H.A.H.A., Mikey talked to herself inside her head, since Margalo seemed to have moved into another dimension.

Something had definitely happened. At her table, Heather McGinty had everybody hanging on to every word that came out of her mouth. They were all looking over at Margalo, and then covering their mouths to hide something—maybe laughter, maybe things they didn't want to be heard saying, although if you asked Mikey, they were making sure Margalo could see that they were maybe laughing, maybe saying private mean things.

As soon as they were seated, Mikey planned to make Margalo explain, but it turned out that she didn't have to ask anything. Margalo didn't even open her lunch bag, and Mikey could see that Margalo had fled to that other dimension to hide out. So instead of demanding answers, Mikey said, "You better take out your lunch."

Margalo obeyed. Then, "Do I have to eat it, too?" she asked.

This was more like Margalo. "Only if it's not something I like," Mikey said. "Is it something I'd want?"

"Cream cheese and jelly."

"What kind of jelly?"

This was a perfectly normal conversation they were having, and anyone watching could see that they were doing what they always did, comparing lunches, trading.

"Grape."

"Crud, Margalo, you know how I feel about grape jelly. Why not strawberry?"

"Grape was on sale."

"On sale at Sam's?"

Margalo nodded.

"So it's what you'll be bringing for a month?" At Sam's Club, you had to buy in quantity. That was part of what made it such a savings to shop there. "Hey, I should join Sam's Club, and Aurora can take me shopping with her for the cookie ingredients."

"You hate shopping."

"Not for food."

"*I* hate shopping for food," Margalo pointed out.

"You can stay home. It'll be a bonding experience for me and Aurora," Mikey said.

That at least made Margalo smile. "She says being alone with you makes her nervous."

"Being alone with me makes *me* nervous."

"I don't get it," Margalo said now. "I just don't—do *you* know what's going on?"

"You're the one who's supposed to be so smart about people," Mikey reminded her.

"I am, but—" Margalo thought, while Mikey watched. Watching, she saw Margalo get angry, deep in her eyes, far behind the outside of her face. Margalo got cold and stony angry, unlike Mikey, who went in for fast and furious.

"It's got to be the sweater," Margalo decided. "But—I don't get it, Mikey. I *know* it's a great sweater, but all of a sudden Heather from Hell looks like she just heard she won the war. Let's get out of here. Hurry and finish. I need to look in a mirror."

But before they could finish, Heather McGinty had come over to their table, with Annie Piers right behind her. The Barbies, at a nearby table, all turned their big-haired heads to watch.

"That's an unusual sweater, Margalo," Heather said. She was carrying half a grilled cheese sandwich and nibbled it.

Mikey remembered how good it felt to take a poke at a face like the one Heather McGinty was wearing. The face hung over her scoop-necked pink jersey shirt, with the little short-sleeved pink blouse over it.

And a little gold chain around her neck so thin, it would probably snap if somebody were to try strangling Heather with it.

Margalo was wary. "Heather. Hihowareyou." Not a question. No answer required. Nobody thought Margalo gave one hoot how Heather was.

Heather smirked happily. "That sweater looks—I don't know anything about this, of course—but it looks *foreign*," Heather said, taking another little nibble. Nibble, nibble. "Where'd you get it?"

Margalo shrugged. With elaborate care, she folded up the wax paper her sandwich had been wrapped in.

"You know," Heather said, all fake surprise as if she had just thought of this, all fake big-eyed wonder, "I bet—is that a La Scala, Margalo? A genuine La Scala?"

Margalo kept cool, but she was surprised. "You've got a good eye."

"Better than you know," Heather said, and turned away, her sandwich at her mouth again, her little white teeth going nibble nibble.

Mikey took a look at Rhonda's happy face at the Barbie table, and at the red back of Ronnie's neck. She saw the way Tanisha was watching Heather lead her pack of followers back to her own table. Something was definitely wrong, and other people knew what it was. She'd *make* Ronnie tell her, or Tan. They both owed her.

"Let's go," Margalo said suddenly. She left the cafeteria, followed by Mikey and many pairs of eyes.

In the bathroom, Margalo studied herself in the mirror. "What is it?" Mikey demanded, and Margalo unbuckled her belt, unbuttoned the sweater, and took it off. In the baggy gray T-shirt, she looked like a skinny kid, any seventh grader. "Can't you tell?" Mikey asked, but Margalo's attention was fixed on the mirror. She put the sweater on, buttoned it up to the top, buckled the belt—and looked like the cover of *Elle* again.

"What are you *doing?*" Mikey demanded. "And what are we going to do about Heather McGinty? She's up to something."

"It *is* a great look," Margalo said, sounding both more puzzled and more confident.

The door opened, two seventh-grade girls looked in, saw who was there, and left. Behind them, four eighth graders entered, talking about Christmas shopping and some boy named Alex.

"Let's get out of here," Margalo said.

She wouldn't talk, but she was thinking hard.

Mikey—for once—just followed Margalo without asking questions. Mikey couldn't think of anything else to do. They lurked among stacks in the library for a while, and then went early to seminar, where they sat together at the long table and played tic-tac-toe until Margalo, at last, announced, "First we have to figure out what's wrong. I did ask Ronnie, before lunch. She said"—Margalo whined the next word—"'nothing.' But her eyes said, *I can't tell*. Ronnie's a rotten liar."

"Ronnie is going to the dogs," Mikey announced, and marked down her X. "What about your new friend Casey, who loaned you her mascara?"

"That was Cassie." Margalo placed an O that gave away the game. "Casey's the one who loaned me a book."

"What about your new friend Casey who didn't loan you her mascara?" Mikey drew another tic-tac-toe grid on the paper. "Why don't you ask *her*?"

"If I did"—Margalo set her O in the center—"she'd probably lie to me, and if she lied to me, then she'd never feel like I could trust her, and she'd know I'd be right not to, and that would make her feel bad, so she'd stop liking me."

"Zooks, Margalo," Mikey said, placing her X in

the corner so the game would play out to a tie and she wouldn't loose.

"Odds bodkins," Margalo agreed, putting her O under Mikey's X.

Mikey quickly marked X in the column opposite, and Margalo put her third O under her second. Mikey put in the deciding X. There was no way Margalo could stop her now. "So how are you going to find out?" she asked, as other members of the seminar entered, Mrs. Brannigan with them.

Margalo shook her head. "I don't know. I can't . . . It's something that when I don't know it, that's the way Heather wants it, so maybe—Maybe we'll never find out," Margalo said.

But Frannie told them.

She told them after school, between homeroom and buses. She told them in the hallway by their lockers. She told them in the middle of everybody, and she told them more than she knew she was telling them.

Frannie came right up to them, looking worried. "Hey, Mikey, hey Margalo. Do you know what they're saying about your sweater, Margalo?"

"No," Margalo said, and, "No," Mikey said, "what?"

"Heather says we shouldn't tell you we know. She thinks if you know we know, you'll be embarrassed."

"Know what?" Margalo asked in a stiff, thin voice, and Mikey said, "I'll embarrass *her*."

"Where you got your sweater," Frannie explained.

"What about where I got my sweater?" Margalo asked, and "So what?" Mikey demanded.

"Heather says it's a sweater her mother's old aunt got in Rome. The aunt and a lot of other old ladies went on a trip to Italy this fall, and she sent Mrs. McGinty this Italian sweater. Mrs. McGinty wouldn't even try it on. She gave it to her cleaning lady. But the cleaning lady didn't want it, either, so she gave it to her church thrift shop. Heather called home at lunch to find out. Today is one of the days their house is cleaned."

"We clean ours on Saturday," Mikey announced. She thought that Margalo was standing so still and stiff that she could probably break her in half between thumb and forefinger, the way you snap a strand of spaghetti. "I vacuum, and Dad mops. When do you clean?" she asked Frannie.

Frannie was not diverted. "I thought someone should tell you," she said. "I thought you ought to . . . know."

"Thank you," Margalo said to Frannie. "Thank you, too," she said to Mikey.

Mikey ignored that. "I think Margalo looks about twenty. Don't you?" she asked Frannie.

"Why would you want to look twenty?" Frannie asked Margalo.

"Like a model," Mikey explained.

"Oh. Well, you do," Frannie said to Margalo. "You don't see many models in junior high. No wonder," she said.

And for some reason, that struck Margalo as funny. She started to laugh, and so did Frannie. Mikey would have liked to join in, but she didn't get it.

"See you. Tomorrow," Frannie said, and went off.

Mikey and Margalo stood with their backs to the hall, and everyone in it. The noise of people moving along, getting books and papers ready to take home on the buses, getting ready to go to locker rooms and change, began to fade behind them. Mikey looked sideways at Margalo, who seemed lost in thought. "Are you taking the late bus today?"

Margalo nodded.

"Doing homework in the library?"

Margalo nodded.

"Do you believe Heather McGinty really wanted to spare your feelings?"

Margalo shook her head.

"Neither do I," Mikey said. "Not for one nanosecond. What are you going to do?"

Margalo shrugged.

Mikey stared into Margalo's face, and eyes. Cold and stony.

Well, okay. Maybe Margalo wasn't going to do anything. But Mikey would. She didn't know what, but she'd think of something—something to make Heather McGinty sorry she'd tried her poison snake tricks on Mikey's friend, Margalo.

A satisfying fury was building up in Mikey's chest. "She's not going to know what hit her," Mikey promised Margalo. "But it's going to be me."

14

Godzilla vs Thumbelina

Mikey greeted Margalo with a question the next day, Thursday. "Who was on the phone at your house all last night?"

Margalo wore a long woolen winter coat on this cold morning, and jeans. She didn't look like a queen anymore, or a model. She looked like someone very far away.

"It wasn't you, was it?" Mikey demanded. "Who would you talk to all night, except me? Anyway, what happened to Aurora and Steven's five-minute rule?"

"Susannah had another fight with her boyfriend," Margalo said, without walking any slower to talk, without turning her head to look at Mikey, "so they had to make up. Aurora canceled the five-minute rule because Susannah has to keep the no-dates-on-school-nights rule."

They were going in to school and then down the hall, both carefully paying no attention to anybody around.

"For liberal types, your parents can be pretty strict," Mikey observed, but Margalo didn't rise to that bait the way she usually would. Mikey said, "You're coming home with me today, aren't you? You have to; we have baking to get done. You said you would."

"Did I say that?" Margalo asked.

"You are, aren't you? You have a note from Aurora, don't you?" Mikey didn't know *what* was going on with Margalo, and that irritated her.

At their lockers, Margalo put some books in, and took some books out, doing nothing about her coat. Mikey didn't want to stare and she didn't want to ask, but she was getting impatient, and she *was* curious—for once, she was interested in what Margalo was wearing to school. Also, she wanted to get to the library, where they could huddle in the stacks and start planning their revenges. It took Mikey about ten seconds to get her books ready for the first morning classes, but Margalo dawdled away, fiddling around with papers and her lunch bag, her back to the hall and everyone in it.

Finally she took off her coat. She took off her coat and folded it up into a thick pillow shape, to store it in the locker. Then she turned around to face Mikey, and anyone else who might be passing by.

Mikey almost cheered. She almost jumped up in the air as if she was wearing a cute little pleated skirt, jumped up in the air and waved her hands as if she was carrying pom-poms, to start off the cheer "Give us an M!"

Because Margalo was wearing that sweater again.

Everything was all right if Margalo was going to wear that same sweater the very next day, and not be squashed by Heather McGinty. It wasn't that Mikey actually thought Heather McGinty could squash Margalo, but suspecting, and guessing, and hoping aren't the same thing as seeing. Seeing, as they say, is believing.

"What?" Margalo demanded. "What's the *matter* with you, Mikey?"

But she knew. She knew exactly what.

Mikey was also glad to see the top of her gray T-shirt showing close around Margalo's neck. She wanted to have a part in this. But what she said was, "Did you wash the T-shirt last night?"

"Who cares?" Margalo was glaring at Mikey.

"Jeez Loueez, Margalo. I'm not the enemy. I was wondering if you want me to bring in another one, so you don't have to wash every night."

"Who says I'm going to wear—" Then Margalo gave in, and grinned back. "Yeah, I'd appreciate that."

"Hey, girl," Tanisha said, coming up, stopping just long enough to punch Margalo gently on the shoulder, moving quickly on.

"Okay, then, what else are you thinking of?" Mikey asked. She had no trouble letting Margalo be boss of this. "For your revenge."

"What revenge?" Margalo asked.

At that point, Cassie interrupted. "You aren't going to let Heather get away with this, are you?" She stepped right in between them, said, "You're Mikey. You make those cookies. I'm Cassie," then turned back to Margalo, her dark eyes dramatic. "We can protest, with signs, with slogans. *Poor and proud of it. Paupers are people, too.* You can count on me," Cassie said, and dashed off.

"Who *are* these people?" Mikey demanded. "You're making too many friends," she accused Margalo, but Margalo was accepting a copy of a paperback book from one of the preppies, a thick book with its pages fanned out the way paperbacks get when they've been read over and over. *The Fellowship of the Ring.*

"I thought you'd like to borrow this. It's my own copy," the girl said, her short brown hair in loose curls, probably natural. Then she was called away and ran down the hall, the sweater she wore tied around her neck swaying on her back.

Mikey reclaimed Margalo's attention by asking, "What are you going to do about Heather?" but Frannie Arenberg stepped up before Margalo could answer.

"I never think it means anything how much money someone has," Frannie told Margalo and Mikey. "Do you? I don't think money's anything more than another difference, like your religion, or race."

"We're not the ones who don't know that," Margalo answered.

Nobody even noticed Mikey. Except Cassie had. Cassie might be okay, Mikey thought.

"I already told Heather," Frannie said.

"You *did?*"

"Of course, why shouldn't I? See you at lunch?" and she ran off.

"I guess you've got some plan all worked out," Mikey said. "So what is it?"

"I plan to ignore it. Pretend it never happened."

"Right," Mikey said. "Sure. I guess that's why you're wearing the sweater again. And probably all the rest of the school year, too, every day. To ignore it."

Margalo smiled. "Otherwise, how will Heather know I don't care? Besides, what else can I do, Mikey? I mean, she's right. I bought this sweater at the New-to-You. It's something her mother threw out. Those things are true, and I can't think of any useful lie to tell about them, not any lie that anyone would begin to believe."

"But—" Mikey said, but Margalo shook her head.

"You're not going to do anything?" Mikey asked.

Margalo nodded her head, then admitted, "I felt so—bad—yesterday."

"Nobody could tell," Mikey assured her.

"With people talking about feeling sorry for me, I felt like—"

"Not me," Mikey said.

"Like I was all shriveled up. I wanted to blow away on some wind, and never have to see anybody I knew ever again." Margalo stopped speaking. Thought. Added, "Except you. You don't feel sorry for me."

"Nope," Mikey agreed. Then, to be honest, she added, "Except about being so tall, and bad at math. And caring about what people think," she added.

216

"That's better than never listening to anybody," Margalo snapped back.

Mikey was so glad to have Margalo back snapping back at her, she couldn't keep up the quarrel. She tried to explain. "I *know* you want to be popular. In fact, I *want* you to be. The more popular you are, the better I look, because I'm your friend. You know that's true, Margalo. And what's so funny?"

Margalo shook her head, trying not to laugh.

Mikey got back to the point. "So you're just going to let Heather get away with it?"

Now Margalo smiled, practically the Mona Lisa. "Do you think she's getting away with it?" Then she got serious. "I thought about it, and all I can do to her is—you know what they say? Living well is the best revenge."

Mikey stuck her tongue out at Margalo. She'd been looking forward to hearing some great plan of Margalo's, for one thing, and for another, whether Margalo wanted to do anything about it or not, Heather *had* tried to humiliate her. So it looked like Mikey was just going to have to take care of Heather on her own.

"Don't you do anything, either," Margalo told Mikey.

As it happened, Heather McGinty, in the midst of her clique, was coming down the hallway in their direction, giggling and talking, her pleated skirt swishing around just above her knees. She made a point of not staring at Mikey and Margalo, although she pointed her face in their direction so they'd be afraid she *might* be staring.

"Okay," Mikey said, soft, out of the side of her mouth. She was looking right at Heather McGinty. "Okay, I won't *do* anything," she said, giving Margalo her word, giving Heather McGinty the kind of look an *If-looks-could-kill* look was named after.

Heather McGinty walked a little faster and found her path down the hallway veering away from the two girls standing by their lockers, one of them short and round and dressed in dumpy cargo jeans, with a baggy gray T-shirt and staring in a not-at-all-nice way; the other tall and skinny, and wearing that same thrift shop sweater.

(Wearing the same sweater? How could she dare to do that?

Maybe she hadn't heard the story, yet.

But then why was Mikey staring like that, like some Doberman pincher about to attack?)

Heather McGinty did not look back over her shoulder as she hustled down the hall.

By lunchtime, Heather was convinced that Mikey

was going to attack her, and maybe beat her up. Although Mikey hadn't done anything. Just smiled.

Mikey didn't need to do anything but smile.

So that when Heather approached her table, lunch tray in her hands, and saw Mikey standing nearby, smiling at her, she put the tray down quickly.

Mikey didn't move. True to her word, she didn't do anything. But Heather found she had to go to the bathroom, and when she came back, Mikey must have finished her lunch because there she was, standing by the doorway. It looked like Mikey was waiting for someone, probably Margalo, because the two of them were practically inseparable. Mikey looked at Heather McGinty, and smiled, and Heather decided maybe she wasn't hungry. Since she wasn't hungry, Heather decided to skip lunch. Since she was skipping lunch, she didn't need to go into the cafeteria after all.

Too often, that Thursday, where Heather wanted to go, Mikey blocked her way. "She's not doing anything," Heather's friends pointed out, but nobody had ever looked at Heather like that. "And sometimes she smiles," Heather said.

"Just stay away from her," they advised. Privately, they thought Heather deserved what she was getting.

"She's stalking me!" Heather cried.

Friday morning, Mikey and Margalo brought in six shoe boxes of chocolate chip cookies in two shopping bags. They followed the same marketing plan, leaving one bag with Mrs. Chambers, setting two boxes under the bake sale table, and leaving one out on top. There was no reason to make changes in a successful strategy, Mikey said. Margalo wore her La Scala sweater again, this time over her long, black skirt.

On her way to the cafeteria for lunch, Margalo lifted the cloth that covered the bake sale table and took a peek underneath, to see that even the third ME shoe box was gone. "Margalo. Hihowareyou?" Annie Piers called to her, from her seat behind the table. Annie leaned around a couple of customers to ask, "Can you help out here? Heather never showed, if you can believe it." So Margalo guessed she knew where Mikey was. She took a seat behind the table and told people, no, there weren't any more of Mikey's chocolate chips, and asked them why didn't they try one of the brownies instead. "Will there be more of Mikey's cookies later? Like last week?" they asked, and she smiled, not saying yes and not saying no.

The anti-Heather campaign continued the next week, through Monday and into Tuesday. Margalo continued to wear the La Scala sweater, and Mikey kept on doing nothing to Heather. On Tuesday, Heather had actually entered the cafeteria, and joined the line, not noticing Mikey crouched beside the table where the jockettes ate. Then Mikey rose up.

Mikey didn't say anything, and she didn't rush, either. In fact, she moved so slowly, one foot in front of the other, that Heather had plenty of time to wonder what was going to happen, and start getting dancey feet where she was standing in line, crowded in by people.

Mikey approached.

Heather backed away, just a little.

Mikey kept coming.

Heather knew that if she fled, people would laugh at her. So she tried to stay where she was, standing in line.

But Mikey was moving steadily closer, like some glacier, silent and unstoppable. Her eyes never left Heather's face. Her grim smile never faltered.

Heather backed up against the utensil rack. "C'mon, Mikey," she said. "Cut it out," she said.

Mikey didn't say one word. Her hands were in her pockets, but there was something about her shoulders . . . She wasn't doing anything, but she might, any minute, start doing something. Something that made her smile to think about, an *If-you-think-it's-bad-now-wait-till-you-see-what's-next* smile.

Heather's hands were in front of her, and her backside was jammed up against the metal rack that held silverware. There was nowhere else for her to go, and Mikey was still getting closer.

Until a large, coppery brown hand fell down on Mikey's shoulder. But even that didn't stop Mikey—who was concentrating harder than she did for anything, except tennis—until a matching large hand fell on the back of her neck, ready to squeeze, and Mr. Saunders said, "Come with me, Mikey."

15
Two (bad) Eggs, Sunny-side Up

"He's not worried about me getting pregnant anymore," Mikey announced with satisfaction.

They were bouncing along homeward on the activities bus. Margalo had had to wait through three afternoon classes and a basketball practice to hear what the principal had said to Mikey. And even now she was having trouble keeping Mikey's attention focused. Mikey kept wanting to talk about basketball. "But I think I know what you have to do on free throws."

"What did he *say?*" Margalo asked, for about the hundredth time. "You were in there for over an hour."

"Most of the time I was waiting outside his office. It's a matter of attitude," Mikey said.

"That's what he said?"

"No, for free throws, mental attitude. Oh, all right," Mikey said as Margalo groaned her frustration. "Since you can't seem to think about anything else. I got called in—*finally*—and I can tell you, I was tired of Mrs. Chambers giving me the fish eye. It turns out, Mrs. McGinty called up to complain. That's one of the things Mr. Saunders said."

"Why do parents do that?"

"If Heather was your daughter, wouldn't you want to call up somebody—anybody?—and complain?"

"And she's a snitch, too."

"Crikey, Margalo. Who did you think she was?" But Mikey couldn't think of any girl or woman courageous, quick-witted, and loyal enough to be the shining example of what Heather McGinty wasn't. She started to grouse at Margalo about that. "Do you realize that there's no girl—"

Margalo couldn't be diverted from this one subject. "What's your punishment?" she asked. "Because I'll help with it. Since it's sort of my fault."

"No punishment."

That shut Margalo up, but only temporarily. Mikey had barely begun telling Margalo her new technique for free throws, when Margalo turned away from the window to interrupt, again. "If he's not worried about your teen pregnancy anymore, what *is* he worried about?

"He's worried I'm a terrorist."

"Not really."

"Not really, and not right now, but—that maybe I might turn into one."

"Well, I can see why he'd think of that, but I don't agree. What did you say?"

"I told him"—Mikey smiled a *You're-going-to-love-this* smile—"'I'm not a terrorist, I'm an entrepreneur.'"

Margalo waited a few seconds before asking, "And what did he say to that?" This was like pulling teeth, getting information. "C'mon, Mikey, what's with you? Just *tell*."

"He said, I was a wise guy. I said, I was just telling the truth. He said, sarcastic, how did I define entrepreneur, and I said—I was very polite, a lot more polite than he was—I defined entrepreneur as someone who tried to create new businesses, and make a lot of money."

Mikey stopped.

Margalo waited, then asked again, "And he said?"

Mikey sighed, but Margalo didn't believe that sigh for one second. "He said, he didn't see much opportunity for new businesses in the seventh grade. And I said"—Mikey beat Margalo to the question— "that was because he wasn't an entrepreneur."

She allowed herself a *Game-set-match* smile.

Margalo grinned right back at her. "So you're not in trouble?"

"Oh, that. Not exactly. He said, 'This has to cease and desist. Is that understood?'" Mikey reported this last in a deep, mock-principal voice. "If I don't, he said, he'll have me pinned to the mat before I know what the name of the game is. I think he forgot he was dealing with a girl," Mikey announced. "So I said, just as nice as Frannie, 'Okay, I will.' And he waited a couple of minutes, sort of looking stern at me across his desk, before he told me I could go. End of story."

"Are you going to cease and desist?" Margalo asked.

"This was already going to be the last day," Mikey told her. "I figured, in four days I would have done all the damage I could."

"He didn't even give you detention?" Margalo asked.

"It isn't as if I actually *did* anything. Or even said anything. Why should I get detention?"

"That's okay, then," Margalo said. She turned back to the window.

It was Mikey's turn to ask, "Do you mind being poor, Margalo?"

Now Margalo sighed, to let Mikey know how tired she was of this topic. "I'm not poor. We just need everything we take in, from Steven's job and the child support Howie and Esther's father sends."

"And from my dad, too."

"From your dad, too."

"But do you *mind?*" Mikey insisted.

Margalo blew up. "Of course I do. Jeez Loueez, Mikey, how dumb can you be? Wouldn't *you* mind if"—she tried to think of an example that would matter to Mikey—"if you had to buy your sneakers at a discount drugstore?"

"But those don't last. They don't stand up to any serious wear. I'm hard on sneakers."

"Or when you wanted to make cookies, if you had to use margarine because it's so much cheaper?"

"But that would change the taste."

"You're missing the point."

Mikey explained, "But you *can't* mind very much, because you've never done anything about it."

"Like what?" Margalo demanded. "Like what can I

227

do? Rob a bank? I'll get a job when I turn fourteen, Aurora promised I can, and she says I can use what I earn for college."

"What *about* California?" Mikey wondered now. Were she and Margalo on such entirely different wavelengths?

"What about California? It's a state. It borders on the Pacific. The capital is Sacramento."

Mikey explained, "You were saving money for a plane ticket to California. For this summer. What is *with* you, Margalo?"

Margalo spoke between clenched teeth. "How can I save money? You have to have money to spend in order to have money to save by not spending it."

Mikey returned to her main point to be sure that now, at least, she was getting it right. "So you do mind." She thought some more. "*Zut*, are you a good actress, Margalo."

"Of course I'm a good actress, you nitwit."

Mikey decided to change the subject, since this one just seemed to get Margalo het up. There was no sense in having a big fight with the only person who liked you at school, except maybe Frannie Arenberg. "What if we try sugar cookies this week? We could make half sugar cookies and half chocolate chip,"

Mikey said, slipping into the satisfying memory. "Because chocolate chip is my trademark."

"Here's the plan," Mikey greeted Margalo the next morning, Wednesday, as she got off her bus, but she was cut off by Margalo insisting that they get inside, out of the heavy rain. "Don't you have a raincoat?" Mikey demanded.

"Lay off, why don't you?" Margalo responded, so Mikey guessed her mood had not improved overnight. Maybe she hadn't gotten enough sleep.

"Here's the plan," Mikey began again, at their lockers—but Margalo wasn't wearing the sweater anymore. She was wearing some flowered blouse, dark browny red printed with big, droopy cream-colored flowers, and a large soft floppy collar that spread almost to her shoulders, a really goopy blouse, in Mikey's opinion.

"Great blouse," somebody said. The somebody was Casey Wolsowski, who now said, "Mikey? Love your cookies. I'm Casey, hihowareyou?"

"Wet," Mikey answered. "Otherwise, pretty good because I got a really good night's sleep. Also, my dad got us bagels for breakfast." She thought about what else Casey might want to know. "I'm staying with my mother this weekend, but I don't start getting jumpy about that until Friday. She likes me better since the divorce, but I'm not exactly her favorite person a lot of the time."

"Oh," Casey said. "Well. That's—Hihowareyou, Margalo?"

"Cool," Margalo said. Whatever that meant, Mikey thought. "You?" Margalo asked.

"Equally. Take me shopping with you sometime, will you?" Casey asked. "I mean it. You come too, Mikey. Gotta go."

Mikey stared at Margalo, who stared right back. "You *could*," Margalo said.

"Who says I want to?" Mikey demanded.

But there was no time for a fight, not even time for a little quarrel, because Tan came up to ask them, "Whazzup?"

"Nothing," Mikey told her. "Nothing ever is. Except, I had this idea about free throws. See, if I—"

Tan shook her head and punched Mikey's shoulder. "Show me in practice. Hey, Margalo, whazzup?"

"Whazzup?" Margalo answered, and Tan waved over her shoulder as she went off.

"So do you want to hear the plan? Or—"

Another interruption, Cassie with blue fingernails.

"Hey, Margalo, Mikey. What's new?"

"Nothing," Mikey said. "This is school, isn't it?"

"It was the last time I looked," Cassie agreed, and Margalo asked her, "What's new with you?"

"Some of us are sick of Heather McGinty," Cassie said. "Probably we'll never speak to her again. Of course, we didn't speak to her before this, either."

"I don't plan to even think about Heather McGinty, ever again," Margalo said. "She's entirely too uninteresting, isn't she, Mikey?"

"I wouldn't say that," Mikey answered. "It's kind of fun to watch her shoot herself in the feet."

Cassie laughed, a sharp, witchy sound. "You're really bad."

Mikey didn't laugh. "I'm really bad," she agreed.

Cassie got serious. "You really *are*." She turned back to Margalo. "Come around sometime. Mikey, too, if she wants," and she went off.

"Come around?" Mikey asked. "Where? What is she *talking* about?"

In the cafeteria, Mikey told Margalo, "I've got an appointment with Mr. Saunders at the end of this lunch. Are you coming with me?" she asked.

Wednesday's lunch was supposed to be Mexican—

231

but the casserole had gotten as far south as maybe Amarillo, and stopped there. Or maybe the casserole was still in Tombstone, waiting for a decent burial.

"I thought he was through with you," Margalo said, unwrapping a grape jelly sandwich, made with mayonnaise and slices of banana.

"So did he. But I have this plan—" Mikey stopped, waiting to be interrupted by somebody coming along to talk to Margalo, but nobody did. "There's not enough time," Mikey said, and took another bite of her lunch. She looked longingly at Margalo's Oreos.

"Not enough time for what?"

"To explain. Do you want to come with me? Or are you too popular?"

"Well," Margalo explained, "it's easier for people to like someone they feel sorry for than someone they admire."

"Are you saying they admire me?"

Margalo nodded, considered taking a bite of her sandwich, stopped to explain. "They admire you about the petition, and the cookies, and that fight with Ralph."

"But I lost the fight."

"Yeah, but you *had* it. My theory is that most people think other people are just one thing. Like, everyone says Frannie is so nice, and that settles her for them. They think *you're* tough."

"I am," Mikey said.

"Yeah, but—you know what I mean. *Everybody's* more than just one thing, I mean."

Mikey swallowed her mouthful of casserole and she pointed out the obvious to Margalo. "You're not most people."

"That's right."

Mikey continued thinking about her friend. "But I am sort of an extreme, aren't I? And so's Frannie, but you're in the middle. You're sort of everything. Do you do that on purpose?" she asked, with admiration. "So nobody can figure you out or know what you're really like?"

"Except, you do," Margalo acknowledged.

"That's right," Mikey agreed, then admitted, "at least, mostly." She seized the opportunity to ask, "Are you coming with me to see Mr. Saunders?"

"I guess I better. If I don't, I'll never find out this new plan of yours." Margalo peeled her orange, and only then did she offer Mikey an Oreo, to dip into her scoop of vanilla ice cream.

"That's because people keep interrupting us, now that we're so popular," Mikey said, and laughed.

"We'll just have to get back on their bad sides again," Margalo said, and grinned. "I bet we can. I bet we could do it in two days. I bet, if Heather hadn't been so dumb, we could have gotten back to being just as unpopular as we were before by the end of the day today."

Frannie joined them, so that they could all go to seminar, and of course she wanted to go with them to the appointment. "Don't tell me anything more, Mikey. I want to be surprised," Frannie said.

Mr. Saunders wasn't surprised to see Mikey enter his office with a couple of henchpersons at her side. "Hello, girls," he greeted them warily. "Mikey."

"Here's the idea," Mikey said. "I want to sell food at the eighth-grade dance."

Mr. Saunders didn't miss a beat. "What would your class need more money for?"

"Not for the class," Mikey said. "For me. And Margalo; she's my partner. I want you to give me the concession."

Mr. Saunders leaned back in his chair, studying her.

"Or I'll rent it from the school," Mikey suggested. "Like they do at a stadium, or a circus."

Mr. Saunders put his fingers together and looked

at Mikey over the top of his finger tent. "I'm not sure that it's appropriate to use school events for private profit," he said.

"Are you sure it's *not* appropriate?" Mikey asked.

"No." He shook his head, and repeated himself. "No."

"Because if it turns out to be, I could always set up outside the building," Mikey offered.

"You'd still be on school property."

"Or on the sidewalk," Mikey said, considering this new idea. "I could do that, and then I could sell to civilians, passersby, too, couldn't I? I'm thinking of some kind of a booth, with a counter, and wheels. It could go anywhere."

"What food are you thinking of selling?" Mr. Saunders asked. "Cookies, of course."

"Maybe individual pizzas; we could heat them in toaster ovens. Pizza is always popular. Sandwiches, probably, too. The refreshments committee will have chips and sodas, inside, that kind of junk food, so I'm not going to do drinks."

"Theirs will be free of charge," Mr. Saunders pointed out.

"Mine will taste good," Mikey pointed out.

Then there was a brief silence. Mr. Saunders nodded

his head, once, briskly, and said, "All right, Mikey. Unless there is some reason, in the fire code or the school building usage rules, I see no problem."

"Good," Mikey said. "Because I'm thinking I might keep the booth, and set up a concession stand during games."

Mr. Saunders looked up quickly.

"That *would* be good publicity for the school, wouldn't it, Mr. Saunders?" Margalo remarked, as if she really was a partner and had already talked all of this over with Mikey. "Parents are always impressed when kids do something on their own, don't you think?"

"We'll see," Mr. Saunders said, then, "I'll see what I can do." He rose from his seat and said, "I'll do my best for you, Mikey."

"That's good enough for me, Mr. Saunders," Mikey said, formally, almost like reaching across the desk for the handshake closing a real business deal.

But Margalo was seized by inspiration. Inspiration got its big, long-fingered hands on her chest and just squeezed the words up into her throat, whispering in her ear that the timing was too perfect to be missed. "Did you want to ask Mr. Saunders about tennis?" she asked Mikey.

Now Mikey was surprised, but Margalo noticed that Mr. Saunders still wasn't.

"The tennis team," he guessed. "Ask me about playing on the West tennis team this spring," he guessed.

"You could talk to her coach at the Y," Margalo suggested.

"And what makes you think I haven't already done that?" he asked.

Margalo knew when to quit. She quit.

They were out of there, and on their way to seminar, with no time for Margalo to get the details of this concession plan out of Mikey, so that she could begin the changes that would make it really good.

They had to wait for the bus ride home to talk. By then, Margalo had had time to think, and do the math, and get some hopes up. "Frannie will tell people about the concession booth," she said. "Everybody will want to be included."

"I don't *want* everyone included," Mikey groused from the window seat. "I don't want any of them." Margalo couldn't expect her to be cheerful, not this afternoon. Her free throws still sucked, and she wasn't nearly tall enough for jump shots. Hop shots was more like it. Basketball was *hard*.

"But you want some other people, sometimes. Like, to sell stuff, and to keep the pizzas coming hot. Who's going to prepare them, have you thought of that? You'll be busy. And you'll probably stink big time as a salesperson."

"You've been thinking about this," Mikey complained.

"Of course, I have. I'm a partner. What does that mean, Mikey?"

"It means you do half the work. And you have to get Aurora to take us to Sam's Club for my shopping. Dad'll loan me seed money, I'm pretty sure of that. Or Mom will; it won't be much, and after that we'll be able to cover our own expenses. Mostly it means you'll have to run everything during the tennis season."

"Does it mean I get half the money?" Margalo asked.

"Half the profits."

"Because you said you could make fifty dollars a gross, didn't you?"

"That was with cost rounded up, and selling for fifty cents apiece. I plan to charge a dollar. At a dollar a cookie, I figure, we'd make $122.40 a gross. In profits. Half for each of us."

"For California," Margalo said. This was math she could do in her head, dividing the price of the plane

ticket—$407, she remembered that—by $60 a sale—
maybe less but maybe more. "That's, like, only seven
sales. That's, like, the dance and there are more than
six home games in the spring sports season and I can
buy my own plane ticket."

"That's what I figure," Mikey said. She didn't need
Margalo saying "thank you."

"I signed up for the baby-sitting course, but it
doesn't start until January," Margalo told Mikey. She
didn't have to say it out loud: "You were right, there
are things I can do." Mikey could figure that out
without being told.

They bounced along, until Mikey said, "I thought
Hadrian might do some advertising posters," and
Margalo said, "What if, instead of trying to make piz-
zas you did something like—sausages in biscuits? Like
Burger King breakfasts, with an electric frying pan?"

"What are you now, the head chef, too?" Mikey
demanded. "I'll do the food, and you can take care of
the rest."

"I thought you said partners," Margalo said. "It
was only a suggestion. You don't *have* to do anything
just because I suggest it. But if I'm a partner, I might
have an idea that you might listen to. Because, otherwise, how can I be good enough to be a partner?"

"Meatballs!" Mikey cried. "Toothpicks!"

It didn't make any sense to Margalo, unless they were new cuss words Mikey was trying out. *Meatballs* was a noncontender, she thought, but *toothpicks* was possible. "I am good enough to be a partner," she pointed out.

"That's why I asked you," Mikey said.

"You didn't ask."

"You know what I mean."

"You actually *need* me, so you better be nice to me."

"I'm making you half of my business, aren't I?"

"That's so I can go to California with you."

"I'm being your friend, aren't I? *Zut!* Margalo. *Alors!* What more do you want?"

Margalo had her answer ready. "I want you to help me with math. So we can both be on high honor roll. And I'll help you with spelling and English." Then she quickly changed the subject. "Are we going to name the business?"

"Why would we—?" Mikey stopped. Thought. "Do you think we should?"

"I think it would be good publicity. What name do you think? The Booth?" she suggested. "The Cookie Place? M&M's?"

"Mikey's," Mikey suggested right back.

240

"Margalo's," Margalo suggested back again.

"Mikey's and Margalo's," Mikey said, and Margalo gave that the raspberry. "At least it doesn't sound like some candy," Mikey pointed out.

"It needs to be something less like what a couple of kids might think of," Margalo said. "Something like— like a café?"

"Mikey's Café?" That sounded dumb, so she tried the other option. "Margalo's Café?" That sounded just as dumb.

"What about Café Mikey? That's sort of French, and French is good for food. Café Margalo? Or, Chez, Chez something."

And they got to it together, at exactly the same time. They said it together, right into one another's face, it was so perfect. They shrieked it out, laughing, as if they were ordinary, normal seventh-grade girls. "Chez ME!"

1/01
16.00

J
Voi

Voigt, Cynthia

It's not easy being BAD